LAUREL-LEAF BOOKS

"Look out!" somebody screamed. I whipped around, and felt the knife slide down my side, cold. It was meant to split me open from throat to gut, but I had moved just in time. It didn't hurt. You can't feel a knife cut, at first.

Biff stood a few feet away from me, laughing like a maniac. He was wiping the blood off the blade on his already-splattered T-shirt. "You are one dead cat, Rusty-James." His voice was thick and funny-sounding, because of his swollen nose. He wasn't dancing around anymore, and you could tell by the way he moved he was hurtin'. But at least he was on his feet, and I wouldn't be much longer. I was cold, and everything looked watery around the edges. I'd been knife cut before, I knew what it felt like to be bleeding bad.

S. E. HINTON wrote her first novel, *The Outsiders*, when she was sixteen. She is also the author of *That Was Then, This Is Now*; *Rumble Fish*; *Tex*; and *Taming the Star Runner*, all available in Laurel-Leaf editions. She is the recipient of the first Young Adult Services Division/*School Library Journal* Author Award, which recognizes authors "whose books have provided young adults with a window through which they can view their world and which will help them to grow and to understand themselves and their role in society." S. E. Hinton lives in Tulsa, Oklahoma, with her husband and son.

RUMBLE FISH

S. E. Hinton

LAUREL-LEAF BOOKS bring together under a single imprint out-standing works of fiction and nonfiction particularly suitable for young adult readers, both in and out of the classroom. Charles F. Reasoner, Professor Emeritus of Children's Literature and Reading, New York University, is consultant to this series.

Published by
Dell Publishing
a division of
Bantam Doubleday Dell Publishing Group, Inc.
666 Fifth Avenue
New York, New York 10103

ISBN: 0-440-97534-4

RL: 5.1

Reprinted by arrangement with Delacorte Press

Printed in the United States of America

Two Previous Editions

November 1989

33

KRI

another one for David

1

I ran into Steve a couple of days ago. He was real surprised to see me. We hadn't seen each other for a long time.

I was sitting on the beach and he come up to me and said, "Rusty-James?"

I said, "Yeah?" because I didn't recognize him right off. My memory's screwed up some.

"It's me," he said. "It's Steve Hays."

Then I remembered and got up, brushing sand off. "Hey, yeah."

"What are you doing here?" he kept saying, looking at me like he couldn't believe it.

"I live here," I said. "What are you doin' here?"

"I'm on vacation. I'm going to college here."

"Yeah?" I said. "What you goin' to college for?"

"I'm going to teach when I get out. High school, probably. I can't believe it! I never thought I'd see you again. And here of all places!"

I figured I had as much chance of being here as he did, even if we were a long way from where we'd seen each other last. People get excited over the weirdest things. I wondered why I wasn't glad to see him.

"You're goin' to be a teacher, huh?" I said. It figured. He was always reading and stuff.

"What do you do here?" he asked.

"Nothin'. Bum around," I answered. Bumming around is a real popular profession here. You could paint, write, barkeep, or bum around. I tried barkeeping once and didn't much like it.

"Lord, Rusty-James," he said. "How long has it been now?"

I thought for a minute and said, "Five or six years." Math ain't never been my strong point.

"How did you get here?" He just couldn't seem to get over it.

"Me and a friend of mine, Alex, a guy I met in the reformatory, we just started knockin' around after we got out. We been here awhile."

"No kidding?" Steve hadn't changed much. He looked about the same, except for the moustache that made him look like a little kid going to a Halloween party. But a lot of people are growing moustaches these days. I never went in for them myself.

"How long were you in for?" he asked. "I never found out. We moved, you know, right after . . ."

"Five years," I said. I can't remember much about it. Like I said, my memory's screwed up some. If somebody says something to remind me, I can remember things. But if I'm left alone I don't seem to be able to. Sometimes Alex'll say something that brings back the reformatory, but mostly he don't. He don't like remembering it either.

"They put me in solitary once," I said, because Steve seemed to be waiting for something.

He looked at me strangely and said, "Oh? I'm sorry."

He was staring at a scar that runs down my side. It looks like a raised white line. It don't get tan, either.

"I got that in a knife fight," I told him. "A long time ago."

"I know, I was there."

"Yeah," I said, "you were."

For a second I remembered the fight. It was like seeing a movie of it. Steve glanced away for a second. I could tell he was trying not to look for the other scars. They're not real noticeable, but they're not that hard to see either, if you know where to look.

"Hey," he said, too sudden, like he was trying to change the subject. "I want you to meet my girl friend. She won't believe it. I haven't seen you since we were thirteen? Fourteen? I don't know though"—he gave me a look that was half kidding and half serious—"you leave other guys' chicks alone?"

"Yeah," I said. "I got a girl."

"Or two, or three?"

"Just one," I said. I like to keep things simple, and God knows even one can get complicated enough.

"Let's meet for dinner somewhere," he said. "We can talk about the good old days. Man, I have come so far since then . . ."

I didn't stop him from naming a time and a place, even though I didn't much want to talk about the good old days. I didn't even remember them.

"Rusty-James," he was saying, "you gave me a real scare when I first saw you. I thought I'd flipped out. You know who I thought you were for a second?"

My stomach clenched itself into a fist, and an old fear started creeping up my backbone.

"You know who you look just like?"

"Yeah," I said, and remembered everything. I could of been really glad to see ol' Steve, if he hadn't made me remember everything.

2

I was hanging out in Benny's, playing pool, when I heard Biff Wilcox was looking to kill me.

Benny's was the hangout for the junior high kids. The high schoolers used to go there, but when the younger kids moved in, they moved out. Benny was pretty mad about it. Junior high kids don't have as much money to spend. He couldn't do much about it except hate the kids, though. If a place gets marked as a hangout, that's it.

Steve was there, and B.J. Jackson, and Smokey Bennet, and some other guys. I was playing pool with Smokey. I was probably winning, since I was a pretty good pool player. Smokey was hacked off because he already owed me some money. He was glad when Midget came in and said, "Biff is lookin' for you, Rusty-James."

I missed my shot.

"I ain't hidin'." I stood there, leaning on my cue, knowing good and well I wasn't going to be able to finish the game. I can't think about two things at the same time.

"He says he's gonna kill you." Midget was a tall, skinny kid, taller than anybody else our age. That was why we called him Midget.

"Sayin' ain't doin'," I said.

Smokey was putting his cue away. "Biff is a mean cat, Rusty-James," he told me.

"He ain't so tough. What's he shook about, anyway?"

"Somethin' you said to Anita at school," Midget said.

"Shoot, I didn't say nothin' but the truth."

I told them what I said to Anita. B.J. and Smokey agreed it was the truth. Steve and Midget turned red.

"Hell," I said. "Now why does he have to go and get shook over somethin' like that?"

I get annoyed when people want to kill me for some stupid little reason. Something big, and I don't mind it so much.

I went up to the counter and got a chocolate

milk. I always drank chocolate milk instead of Coke or something. That Coke junk will rot your insides. This gave me a little time to think things over. Benny was making a big production out of a sandwich, and he let me know he wasn't going to drop what he was doing and rush over with my chocolate milk.

"So what's he doin' about it? Killin' me, I mean."

I sat down at a booth and Midget slid in across from me. Everybody else gathered around.

"He wants you to meet him in the vacant lot behind the pet store."

"All right. I guess he's comin' alone, huh?"

"I wouldn't count on it," Smokey said. He was trying to let me know he was on my side, so I'd forget about our messed-up pool game.

"If he's bringin' friends, I'm bringin' friends." I wasn't afraid of fighting Biff, but I didn't see any need to be stupid about it.

"Yeah, but you know how that's gonna turn out," Steve put in. "Everybody'll end up gettin' into it. You bring people, he brings people ..."

Steve was always cautious about things.

"You think I'm goin' to that empty lot by myself, you're nuts," I told him.

"But—"

"Lookit, me an' Biff'll settle this thing ourselves. You guys'll just be an audience, huh? Ain't nothin' wrong with an audience."

"You know it ain't gonna end up like that." Steve was fourteen, like me. He looked twelve. He acted forty. He was my best friend, though, so he could say stuff that I wouldn't let anybody else get away with. "Dammit, Rusty-James, we haven't had any trouble like that for a long time now."

He was scared it was going to end up in a gang fight. There hadn't been a real honest-to-goodness gang fight around here in years. As far as I knew, Steve had never been in one. I could never understand people being scared of things they didn't know nothing about.

"You don't have to be there," I said. Everybody else had to be there to protect their rep. Steve didn't have any rep. He was my best friend. That was his rep.

"You know I'm gonna be there," he said to me angrily. "But you know what the Motorcycle Boy said about gang—"

"He ain't here," I said. "He ain't been here for two weeks. So don't go tellin' me about the Motorcycle Boy."

B.J. spoke up. "But even back when we was

rumblin', we never fought Biff's gang. They was allies. Remember when Wilson got jumped over on the Tigers' turf ..."

This started a discussion on who had been jumped, when and where and why. I didn't need to think about that—I had all those records straight in my head anyway. But I did need to think about how I was going to fight Biff, so I wasn't listening much when somebody said, "Anyway, when the Motorcycle Boy gets back—"

I jumped up and slammed my fist down on the table so hard, the table in the next booth rattled and Benny stopped whistling and making his sandwich. Everybody else sat like they was holding their breath.

"The Motorcycle Boy ain't back," I said. I can't see good when I get mad, and my voice was shaking. "I don't know when he's comin' back, if he's comin' back. So if you wanna wait around the rest of your life to see what he says, okay. But I'm gonna stomp Biff Wilcox's guts tonight, and I think I oughta have some friends there."

"We'll be there," Smokey said. He stared at me with those funny, colorless eyes that gave him his nickname. "But let's try an' keep it between you two, okay?"

I couldn't say anything because I was too mad.

I walked out and slammed the door behind me. In about five seconds I heard footsteps behind me and I didn't turn around because I knew it'd be Steve.

"What's the matter with you?" he said.

"Give me a cigarette."

"You know I don't have any cigarettes."

"Yeah, I forgot."

I hunted around and found one in my shirt pocket.

"What's wrong?" Steve asked again.

"Nothin's wrong."

"Is it the Motorcycle Boy being gone?"

"Don't start in on me," I said. He kept quiet for a few minutes. He'd pestered me once before when he shouldn't of and I'd punched the wind out of him. I was real sorry about that, but it wasn't my fault. He should have known better than to pester me when I'm mad.

Finally he said, "Slow down, willya? You're running my legs off."

I stopped. We were on the bridge, right where the Motorcycle Boy used to stop to watch the water. I threw my cigarette butt into the river. It was so full of trash that a little more wasn't going to hurt it any.

11

"You've been acting funny ever since the Motorcycle Boy left."

"He's been gone before," I said. I get mad quick, and I get over it quick.

"Not for this long."

"Two weeks. That ain't long."

"Maybe he's gone for good."

"Shut up, willya," I said. I closed my eyes. I'd been out till four in the morning the night before and I was kind of tired.

"This is a crummy neighborhood," Steve said suddenly.

"It ain't the slums," I told him, keeping my eyes shut. "There's worse places."

"I didn't say it was the slums. I said it was a crummy neighborhood, and it is."

"If you don't like it, move."

"I am. Someday I am."

I quit listening. I don't see any sense in thinking about things far off in the future.

"You have to face the fact that the Motorcycle Boy may be gone for good."

"I don't have to face nothin'," I said tiredly.

He sighed and stared down at the river.

I saw a rabbit once at the zoo. My old man took me there on the bus a long time ago. I really liked that zoo. I tried to go again by myself, but I was a little kid and I got lost when I had to change buses. I never did get around to trying to get there again. But I remembered it pretty good. The animals reminded me of people. Steve looked like a rabbit. He had dark-blond hair and dark-brown eyes and a face like a real sincere rabbit. He was smarter than me. I ain't never been a particularly smart person. But I get along all right.

I wondered why Steve was my best friend. I let him hang around and kept people from beating him up and listened to all his worries. God, did that kid worry about things! I did all that for him and sometimes he did my math homework and let me copy his history stuff, so I never flunked a grade. But I didn't care about flunking, so that wasn't why he was my best friend. Maybe it was because I had known him longer than I'd known anybody I wasn't related to. For a tough kid I had a bad habit of getting attached to people.

3

When Steve had to go home I went over to my girl friend's place. I knew she'd be home because her mother was a nurse and worked nights and Patty had to take care of her little brothers.

"I'm not supposed to have company when Mother's out." She stood there blocking the doorway, not making a move to let me in.

"Since when?"

"Since a long time ago."

"Well, that ain't stopped you before," I said. She was mad about something. She wanted to start a fight. She wasn't mad about me coming over when I wasn't supposed to, but that was what she wanted to fight about. It seemed like whenever we had fights it was never over what she was mad about.

"I haven't seen you in a long time," she said coldly.

"I been busy."

"So I heard."

"Aw, come on," I said. "Let's talk about it inside."

She looked at me for a long time, then held the door open. I knew she would. She was crazy about me.

We sat and watched TV for a while. Patty's little brothers took turns jumping up and down on the only other chair in the room.

"What were you busy with?"

"Nothin'. Messin' around. Me and Smokey and his cousin went to the lake."

"Oh, yeah? Did you take any girls with you?"

"What're you talkin' about, take any girls? No."

"Okay," she said, settling down in my arms. When we started making out, one of the brats started yelling, "I'm gonna tell Mama," until I promised to knock his block off. But after that I just sat there holding her and sometimes kissed the top of her hair. She had blond hair with dark roots. I like blond girls. I don't care how they get that way.

"Rusty-James," she said.

I jumped. "Was I asleep?"

The room was dark, except for the black-and-white glare from the TV.

"Is it morning or night?" I was confused. I still felt like I was asleep or something.

"Night. Boy, you've been great company."

I felt shivery. Then I remembered.

"What time is it?"

"Seven thirty."

"Hell," I said, getting up. "I'm supposed to fight Biff Wilcox at eight. You got anything to drink around here?"

I went into the kitchen and hunted through her refrigerator. I found a can of beer and gulped it down.

"Now Mama'll think I drank it. Thanks a lot." She sounded like she was going to cry.

"What's the matter, honey?" I said.

"You said you were going to quit fighting all the time."

"Since when?"

"Since you beat up Skip Handly. You promised me you wouldn't be fighting all the time."

"Oh, yeah. Well, this ain't all the time. This is just once."

"You always say that." She was crying. I backed

her up against the wall and hugged her awhile.

"Love you, babe," I said, and turned her loose.

"I wish you wouldn't fight all the time." She wasn't crying anymore. She could quit crying the easiest of any girl I knew.

"Well, what about you?" I asked. "You took after Judy McGee with a busted pop bottle not too long ago."

"She was flirting with you," she said. Patty was a hellcat sometimes.

"Ain't my fault," I said. I grabbed my jacket on the way to the door. I stopped and gave her a good long kiss. Pretty little thing, she looked like a dandelion with her hair messed up.

"Be careful," she said. "I love you."

I waved good-bye and jumped off the porch. I thought maybe I'd have time to stop by my place and have a good swig of wine, but going by Benny's I saw everybody waiting around for me, so I went in.

There were more people there than had been there in the afternoon. I guess word had gotten around.

"We just about give up on you," Smokey said.

"Better watch out or I'll take you on for a warm-up," I warned him. I counted the guys and decided maybe six of them would show up at the

17

lot. I didn't see Steve, but didn't worry about it. He couldn't get out much at night.

"Split up and meet me there," I told them, "or we'll have the cops on our tail."

I left with Smokey and B.J. I felt so good. I love fights. I love how I feel before a fight, kind of high, like I can do anything.

"Slow down," B.J. said. "You'd better be savin' your energy."

"If you wasn't so fat you could keep up."

"Don't start that stuff again," B.J. said. He was fat, but he was tough, too. Tough fat guys ain't as rare as you'd think.

"Man, this is just like the old days, ain't it?" I said.

"I wouldn't know," Smokey said. Fights made him edgy. Before a fight he'd get quieter and quieter, and it always bugged the hell out of him that I'd get louder and louder. We had a funny kind of tension between us anyway. He would have been number-one tough cat in our neighborhood if it wasn't for me. Sometimes I could tell he was thinking about fighting me. So far, either he was scared or wanted to stay friends.

"Yeah," I said, "that's right. It was all over before you got into it."

"Hell, that gang stuff was out of style when you

was ten years old, Rusty-James," he told me.

"Eleven. I can remember it. I was in the Little Leaguers."

The Little Leaguers was the peewee branch of the local gang, the Packers. Gang stuff was out of style now.

"Man," I said, "a gang really meant somethin' back then."

"Meant gettin' sent to the hospital once a week."

Okay, so he was edgy. So was I. I was the one doing the fighting, after all. "You're almost talkin' chicken, Smokey," I said.

"I'm almost talkin' sense."

I kept quiet. It took a lot of self-control, but I kept quiet. Smokey got nervous, since quiet ain't my natural state.

"Lookit," he said, "I'm goin', ain't I?"

I guess the thought that he was really going made him brave again, 'cause he went on: "If you think this is gonna turn out to be a rumble, you're crazy. You and Biff are gonna go at it and the rest of us is gonna watch. I doubt too many's gonna show up for that much."

"Sure," I said, only half listening to him. We had come to the pet store. We turned into the alley that ran alongside of it, crawled through a hole in the back fence and came out onto the vacant lot that led right down to the river. The lot was damp and it stank. The area around here always stinks from that river, but it's worse in the lot. Further down, a bunch of plants and factories dump their garbage into the water. You don't notice the stink if you live there awhile. It's just extra strong in that lot.

Smokey was right—only four of the guys who were in Benny's were there waiting for us. B.J. looked around and said, "I thought Steve was gonna be here." He said it sarcastic. They never could understand why I let Steve hang around.

"So, maybe he's late," I said. I didn't really expect him to show up, except that he said he would.

Across the field was Biff and his gang. I counted them, just like the Motorcycle Boy taught me to. Know everything you can about the enemy. There was six. Even enough. I was getting so high on excitement I couldn't stand still.

"Rusty-James! "

It was Biff, coming across the lot to meet me. Oh, man, I couldn't wait. I was going to stomp him good. It seemed like my fists ached to be pounding something. "I'm here!" I called.

"Not for long, you punk," Biff said. He was

close enough for me to see him clearly. My eyes get supersharp before a fight. Everything gets supersharp before a fight—like with a little effort I could fly. During a fight, though, I almost go blind; everything turns red.

Biff was sixteen, but not any bigger than me; husky; his arms hung off his shoulders like an ape's. He had a pug-ugly face and wiry blond hair. He was dancing around worse than I was.

"He's been poppin' pills," Smokey said behind me.

Now, I hate fighting hopped-up people. They're crazy. You get crazy enough in a fight without being doped up. You fight some cat who's been washing down bennies with sneaky pete and they can't tell if you kill 'em. Your only advantage is a little more control. I never do dope, as a rule. Dope ruined the gangs.

Biff looked high. The light from the streetlamps was bouncing off his eyes in a way that made him look crazy.

"I hear you're lookin' for me," I said. "Here I am."

I've done this lots of times before. I'd get in a fight about once a week. I hadn't lost a fight in almost two years. But Biff was a little tougher than the usual kid. If the gang wars had still been going on he would have been leader of the Devilhawks. He didn't like anybody to forget that, either. You can't take it for granted you're going to stomp some snotty-nosed seventh-grader, so when you go up against somebody like Biff Wilcox you think about it.

We started in on the warm up, cussing each other out, name-calling, threats. This was according to the rules. I don't know who made up the rules.

"Come on," I said finally. I like to get down to business. "Take a swing at me."

"Take a swing at you?" Biff's hand went to his back pocket and came out flashing silver. "I'm gonna cut you to ribbons."

I didn't have a knife with me. Most people didn't knife-fight these days. I usually carried a switchblade, but I got caught with it at school and they took it away from me and I hadn't gotten around to getting another one. Biff should of told me it was going to be knife-fighting. God that made me mad! People don't pay attention to the rules anymore.

Biff's friends were cheering and screaming and my friends were grumbling and I said, "Anybody lend me a blade?" I still thought I could win— Biff wouldn't have pulled a knife if he thought he could win in a fair fight. All I had to do was equal things up.

Nobody had a knife. That's what comes of not gang-fighting. People are never prepared.

Somebody said, "Here's a bike chain," and I held back my hand for it, never taking my eyes off Biff.

Just like I expected, he tried to make the most of that moment, lunging at me. I was quick enough, though, grabbing the chain, dodging the knife, and sticking out my foot to trip him. He just stumbled, and whirled around, jabbing at me. I sucked in my gut and wrapped the chain around his neck, jerking him to the ground. All I wanted to do was get the knife away from him. I'd kill him later. First things first. I jumped on top of him, caught his arm as he swung the knife at me, and for what seemed like hours we wrestled for that knife. I took a risk I thought was worth taking and tried holding his knife hand with one arm, and used the other to smash his face. It worked, he loosened his hold on the knife long enough for me to get it away from him. It fell a few feet away from us, far enough away that I didn't bother trying to reach for it, which was good. If I had gotten a hold of it, I'd have killed Biff. As it was, I was pounding his brains out. If he'd give up on that damned knife he might of stood a chance; he was older than me, and just as tough. But he didn't come there to fight fair, so instead of fighting back, he'd just keep trying to get away and crawl over to the knife. Gradually I started to calm down, the red tinge to everything went away, I could hear everyone screaming and yelling. I looked at Biff. His whole face was bloody and swollen.

"You give?" I sat back on his gut and waited. I wouldn't trust him as far as I could throw him. He didn't say anything, just lay there breathing heavy, watching me out of the one eye that wasn't swollen shut. Everybody was quiet. I could feel his gang tensed, ready, like a dog pack about to be set loose. One word from Biff would do it. I glanced over to Smokey. He was ready. My gang would fight, even if they weren't crazy about the idea.

Then a voice I knew said, "Hey, what's this? I thought we signed a treaty." The Motorcycle Boy was back. People cleared a path for him. Everybody was quiet.

I got to my feet. Biff rolled over and lay a few feet away from me, swearing.

"I thought we'd stopped this cowboys and Indians crap," said the Motorcycle Boy.

I heard Biff dragging himself to his feet, but didn't pay any attention. Usually I'm not that stupid, but I couldn't take my eyes off the Motorcycle Boy. I'd thought he was gone for good. I was almost sure he was gone for good.

"Look out!" somebody screamed. I whipped around, and felt the knife slide down my side, cold. It was meant to split me open from throat to gut, but I had moved just in time. It didn't hurt. You can't feel a knife cut, at first.

Biff stood a few feet away from me, laughing like a maniac. He was wiping the blood off the blade on his already-splattered T-shirt. "You are one dead cat, Rusty-James." His voice was thick and funny-sounding, because of his swollen nose. He wasn't dancing around anymore, and you could tell by the way he moved he was hurtin'. But at least he was on his feet, and I wouldn't be much longer. I was cold, and everything looked watery around the edges. I'd been knife cut before, I knew what it felt like to be bleeding bad.

The Motorcycle Boy stepped out, grabbed Biff's wrist and snapped it backwards. You could hear it crack like a matchstick. It was broke, sure enough.

The Motorcycle Boy picked up Biff's switchblade, and looked at the blood running down over the handle. Everybody was frozen. They knew what he had said about gang-fighting being over with.

"I think," he said thoughtfully, "that the show is over."

Biff held his wrist with his other arm. He was swearing, but softly, under his breath. The others were leaving, breaking up into twos and threes, edging away, leaving quieter than you'll ever see people leave a battle ground.

Steve was there beside me. "You okay?"

"When did you get here?" Smokey asked him. Then, to me, he said, "You're hurt, man."

The Motorcycle Boy stood behind them, tall and dark like a shadow.

"I thought you were gone for good," I said.

He shrugged. "So did I."

Steve picked up my jacket, where I'd thrown it on the ground. "Rusty-James, you better go to the hospital."

I looked down at my hand, where it was clutching my side. I saw Smokey Bennet watching me.

"For this?" I said scornfully. "This ain't nothin'."

"But maybe you better go home," the Motorcycle Boy said.

I nodded. I threw an arm across Steve's shoulders. "I knew you was gonna show up."

He knew I would have fallen down if I wasn't leaning on him, but he didn't show it. He was a good kid, Steve, even if he did read too much.

"I had to sneak out," Steve said. "They'd kill me if they knew. Boy, I thought Biff was gonna kill you."

"Not me. It was Biff who was gonna get killed."

I could feel the Motorcycle Boy laughing. But then, I never expected to fool him. I tried not to lean on Steve too much. Smokey walked along with us until we came to his block. I guess I had convinced him I wasn't going to drop dead.

"Where ya been?" I asked the Motorcycle Boy. He'd been gone for two weeks. He had stolen a cycle and left. Everybody called him the Motorcycle Boy because he was crazy about Motorcycles. It was like a title or something. I was probably one of the few people on the block who knew what his real name was. He had this bad habit of borrowing cycles and going for rides without telling the owner. But that was just one of the things he could get away with. He could get away with anything. You'd think he'd have a cycle of his own by now, but he never had and never would. It seemed like he didn't want to own anything.

"California," he said.

"No kiddin'?" I was amazed. "The ocean and everything? How was it?"

"Kid," he said to me, "I never got past the river."

I didn't understand what he meant. I spent a lot of time trying to understand what he meant. It was like the time, years ago, when our gang, the Packers, was having a big rumble with the gang next door. The Motorcycle Boy—he was president —said, "Okay, let's get it straight what we're fighting for."

And everybody was all set to kill or be killed, raring to go, and some cat—I forget his name, he's in prison now—said, "We're fighting to own this street."

And the Motorcycle Boy said, "Bull. We're fighting for fun."

He always saw things different from everybody else. It would help me a lot if I could understand what he meant.

We climbed up the wooden stairs that went up the outside of the dry cleaners to our apartment. Steve eased me onto the platform railing. I hung over the railing and said, "I ain't got my key," so the Motorcycle Boy jimmied the lock and we went on in.

"You better lay down," he said. I laid down on

the cot. We had a mattress and a cot to lay down on. It didn't matter which.

"Boy, are you bleeding!" Steve said.

I sat up and pulled off my sweatshirt. It was soggy with blood. I threw it over into the corner with the other dirty clothes and inspected my wound. I was gashed down the side. It was deep over my ribs; I could see white bone gleaming through. It was a bad cut.

"Where's the old man?" asked the Motorcycle Boy. He was going through the bottles in the sink. He found one with some wine still in it.

"Take a swallow," he told me. I knew what was coming. I wasn't looking forward to it, but I wasn't scared either. Pain don't scare me much.

"Lay down and hang on."

"The old man ain't home yet," I said, laying down on my good side and grabbing hold of the head of the cot.

The Motorcycle Boy poured the rest of the wine over the cut. It hurt like hell. I held my breath and counted and counted and counted until I was sure I could open my mouth without yelling.

Poor Steve was white. "God, that must hurt," he whispered.

"Ain't all that bad," I said, but my voice came out hoarse and funny.

"He oughta go to a doctor," Steve said. The Motorcycle Boy sat down against the wall. He had an expressionless face. He stared at Steve till the poor kid wiggled. The Motorcycle Boy wasn't seeing him, though. He saw things other people couldn't see, and laughed when nothing was funny. He had strange eyes—they made me think of a two-way mirror. Like you could feel somebody on the other side watching you, but the only reflection you saw was your own.

"He's been hurt worse than this," said the Motorcycle Boy. That was the truth. I got cut bad two or three years before.

"But it could get infected," Steve said.

"And they'd have to cut my side off," I added. I shouldn't have teased him. He was only trying to help.

The Motorcycle Boy just sat and stared and stayed quiet.

"He looks different," Steve said to me. Sometimes the Motorcycle Boy went stone deaf—he'd had a lot of concussions in motorcycle wrecks.

I looked at him, trying to figure out what was different. He didn't seem to see either one of us watching him.

"The tan," Steve said.

"Yeah, well, I guess you get tan in California," I said. I couldn't picture the Motorcycle Boy in California, by the ocean. He liked rivers, not oceans.

"Did you know I got expelled from school?" the Motorcycle Boy said out of the clear blue sky.

"How come?" I started to sit up, and changed my mind. They were always threatening to expel me. They'd suspended me for carrying that knife. But the Motorcycle Boy never gave them any trouble. I talked to a guy in one of his classes, once. He said the Motorcycle Boy just sat there and never gave them any trouble, except that a couple of the teachers couldn't stand for him to stare at them.

"How come you got expelled?" I asked.

"Perfect tests."

You could always feel the laughter around him, just under the surface, but this time it came to the top and he grinned. It was a flash, like lightning, far off.

"I handed in perfect semester tests." He shook his head. "Man, I can understand that. A tough district school like that, they got enough to put up with."

31

I was surprised. I don't surprise easy. "But that ain't fair," I said finally.

"When the hell did you start expecting anything to be fair?" he asked. He didn't sound bitter, only a little bit curious.

"Be back in a while," he said, getting to his feet.

"I forgot he was still in school," Steve said after he left. "He looks so old, I forget he's just seventeen."

"That's pretty old."

"Yeah, but he looks really old, like twenty-one or something."

I didn't say anything. I got to thinking—when the Motorcycle Boy was fourteen, that had seemed old. When he was fourteen, like me, he could buy beer. They quit asking for his ID at fourteen. He was president of the Packers then, too. Older guys, eighteen years old, would do anything he said. I thought it would be the same way for me. I thought I would be really big-time, junior high and fourteen. I thought it would be really neat, being that old—but whenever I got to where he had been, nothing was changed except he'd gone further on. It should of been the same way for me.

"Steve," I said, "bring me the old man's shavin' mirror. It's over there by the sink."

When he handed it to me I studied the way I looked.

"We look just like each other," I said.

"Who?"

"Me an' the Motorcycle Boy."

"Naw."

"Yeah, we do."

We had the same color of hair, an odd shade of dark red, like black-cherry pop. I've never seen anybody else with hair that color. Our eyes were the same, the color of a Hershey bar. He was six foot one, but I was getting there.

"Well, what's the difference?" I said finally. I knew there was a difference. People looked at him, and stopped, and looked again. He looked like a panther or something. Me, I just looked like a tough kid, too big for my age.

"Well," Steve said—I liked that kid, he'd think about things—"the Motorcycle Boy . . . I don't know. You can never tell what he's thinking. But you can tell exactly what *you're* thinking."

"No kiddin'?" I said, looking in the mirror. It had to be something more than that.

"Rusty-James," Steve said, "I gotta go home. If

they find out I'm gone, I'm gonna get killed, man. Killed."

"Aw, stick around awhile." I was scared he would go. I can't stand being by myself. That is the only thing I am honest-to-God scared of. If nobody was at home, I would stay up all night out on the streets where there was some people. I didn't mind being cut up. I just couldn't stay there by myself and I wasn't too sure I could walk.

Steve shifted around, uneasy-like. He was one of the few people who knew about that hang-up. I don't go around telling people.

"Just for a little bit," I told him. "The old man oughta be back pretty soon."

"Okay," he said finally. He sat down where the Motorcycle Boy had been sitting. After a while I was kind of dozing off and on. It seemed like I went through the whole fight again in slow motion. I knew I was sort of asleep, but I couldn't stop dreaming.

"I never thought he'd go clear to the ocean," I said to Steve. But Steve wasn't there. The Motorcycle Boy was there, reading a book. He always read books. I'd thought when I got older it'd be easy for me to read books, too, but I knew by now it never would.

It was different when the Motorcycle Boy read books, different from Steve. I don't know why.

The old man was home, snoring away on the mattress. I wondered who'd gotten home first. I couldn't tell what time it was. The lights were still on. I can't tell what time it is when I sleep with the lights on.

"I thought you was gone for good," I said to him.

"Not me." He didn't look up from his page, and for a second I thought I was still dreaming. "I get homesick."

I made a list in my head of people I liked. I do that a lot. It makes me feel good to think of people I like—not so alone. I wondered if I loved anybody. Patty, for sure. The Motorcycle Boy. My father, sort of. Steve, sort of. Then I thought of people I thought I could really count on, and couldn't come up with anybody, but it wasn't as depressing as it sounds.

I was so glad the Motorcycle Boy came home. He was the coolest person in the whole world. Even if he hadn't been my brother he would have been the coolest person in the whole world.

And I was going to be just like him.

4

I went to school the next day. I wasn't feeling too hot and I was bleeding off and on, but I usually go to school if I can. I see all my friends at school.

I got there late and had to go get a late pass and ended up missing math. So I didn't know Steve was absent till lunch and he didn't show up. I asked around about him—Jeannie Martin told me he didn't come to school because his mother had a stroke or something. I worried about that awhile. I hoped it wasn't him sneaking out of the house that give her the stroke. His parents were kind of weird. They never let him do anything.

Jeannie Martin wasn't too thrilled to talk to me. She liked Steve. Poor kid. He wouldn't believe that her tipping his chair over in English meant she liked him. He was still funny about girls. And him fourteen, too! Anyway, she liked him and didn't like me because she thought I'd turn him into a hood. Fat chance. I'd known him since I don't remember when, and nobody thought he was a hood. Try and tell her that.

So I went to the basement and played poker with B.J. and Smokey and lost fifty cents.

"You guys must cheat," I told them. "I can't have rotten luck all the time."

B.J. grinned at me and said, "Naw, you're just a lousy poker player, Rusty-James."

"I ain't either."

"Yeah, you are. Every time you get a good hand, we can tell it. Every time you get a bad hand, we can tell. You ain't gonna earn your livin' gamblin', man."

"Don't give me that. Them cards was marked." I knew they weren't, but I didn't believe that garbage B.J. was giving me. He just wanted to crow about winning.

In gym I just stood around watching basketball practice. I wasn't about to do any basketball. Coach Ryan finally asked me why, and I said I didn't feel like it. I thought I could leave it at that. Coach Ryan was all the time trying to be friends with me. He let me get away with murder. It was like he'd be a big shot, being friends with me, like he owned a vicious dog or something.

"Rusty-James," he said, after looking around, making sure nobody could hear us. "Want to earn a quick five bucks?"

I just looked at him. You never know.

"Price has been giving me a lot of trouble these days."

"Yeah," I said. Don Price was a smart alec. Real mouthy. I'm mouthy, too, but I don't mean nothing by it. He was mouthy just to get on people's nerves. A real obnoxious kid.

"I'll give you five bucks to beat him up."

Well, that would have been simple enough. I knew where the guy lived, I could jump him some afternoon. With my rep nobody'd think to ask why. He was just the kind of jerk I liked beating up.

About six months before, a guy had offered the Motorcycle Boy four hundred dollars to kill somebody. That is the truth. He didn't take it. Said whenever he killed somebody it wouldn't be for money.

"I can't fight for a while," I said. I jerked up my gym shirt to show him why.

"Hey, man!" There he was, thirty years old,

saying "Hey, man." He wasn't brought up talking like that, either.

"You been to the nurse?"

"Nope." I pulled my shirt back down. "Ain't gonna, either."

"Well," he said slowly, "let me know when you're healed up."

"Sure thing," I said, and went back to watching practice. He must have thought I needed money real bad.

English was my last class. I liked it because our teacher thought we were so stupid that all she had to do was read us stories. That was all right with me. By the end of the day I was ready to sit still awhile anyway. She didn't have any way of knowing if we were listening. Sometimes she'd give us a test at the end of class, but I could always copy off somebody, if anybody knew the answers.

I'm always in dumb classes. In grade school they start separating dumb people from smart people and it only takes you a couple of years to figure out which one you are. I guess it's easier on the teachers that way, but I think I might like to get in a class with some different people sometimes instead of the same old dummies every year.

Steve was in my math class this year only because he had a choice of new math or business math and he took business math. All the other smart people took new math, but he wasn't crazy about numbers. I'd been going to the same school with him since kindergarten and this was the first year we were in a class together. I wondered if he got tired of seeing the same old smart people every year.

I sat there and didn't listen and thought maybe I'd go by and see Patty after school. If I hadn't lost that fifty cents at lunchtime I could have bribed her brothers to go to the park or something.

Smokey must have been cheating. I ain't that bad a player.

When I went by her house, though, her mother's car was still there. Maybe it was her day off. I never could keep them straight. Her mother wasn't crazy about me. I think the brothers sometimes squealed on Patty. Man, I wanted to knock their blocks off.

So I went to Benny's and shot a game of pool by myself. There were other people there, but nobody playing pool. Everybody who came in wanted to see my knife cut. They thought it was cool.

Steve came by after an hour. I could tell he

wasn't in a mood to hang around Benny's. He just wanted some company, so I left with him.

"How's your old lady?" I asked him after we'd walked a couple of blocks.

"Real sick." He had a funny white look on his face. "She's in the hospital."

"It wasn't you sneakin' out that did it?"

He looked at me like I was off my rocker. Then he remembered and said, "No, it wasn't that."

He didn't say anything else, so I started telling him how Coach Ryan had asked me to beat up a guy. Only I said he offered me fifty dollars to do it, and said I was really thinking about it. But even that didn't seem to shake him out of it. He just said, "Yeah?" like he was somewhere else.

I was needing some money. My old man, he got a regular check from the government. He had to go down and sign for it, but it wasn't very much and sometimes he'd forget to give me some of it before he drank it up. I did a lot of scrounging around. Once in a while I'd borrow money from the Motorcycle Boy, but I had to be really careful and pay it back. I don't know why I was so careful about that. One time he gave me a hundred-dollar bill because he said he didn't want it. I don't know where he got it. Since he didn't want it I didn't worry about paying that back. Most of the time I paid him back, though.

So when I spotted a set of real cool simulated mags on a late-model Chevy, I saw a quick way to make twenty bucks. Twenty dollars would last me a good long while.

The car was sitting there in front of an apartment house, but nobody was around. I had three of the hubcaps off and was working on the fourth one when Steve said, "What are you doing?" like an idiot. I had handed him those three hubcaps and he was standing there asking me what I was doing. I had to work a little harder on the fourth and was getting nervous, so I said, "Shut up."

"You know I don't steal things."

"You know I *do*," I answered. Finally it came off.

Just then three guys came shooting out of that apartment house hollering at us. I took two running steps and saw Steve just standing there, so I had to waste some breath screaming, "Move it!" before he woke up and ran. About two blocks later he realized he was still carrying the hubcaps and threw them down, the dummy. That wasn't going to stop those guys.

They had been swearing at us, but were saving their breath. One stopped to get the hubcaps; I

figured one wouldn't do me any good and threw
mine away a block later. That stopped another
one. The third guy kept on after us.

Steve was keeping up better than I thought he
would, but my side was killing me. I turned down
an alley and cut across a fence. Steve followed
with a desperate look on his face that made me
want to laugh.

The fence slowed down that guy who was chasing us, but it didn't stop him. Man, he was out for
blood. I ran into an apartment house and shot up
the stairs, got to the top and ran out onto the roof.
It was a good-sized jump to the next roof, but I
made it easy. I was tearing off across it for the
next one, when I noticed Steve wasn't with me.

He had stopped at the gap between roofs. He
was almost doubled over from trying to catch his
breath.

"Come on," I said. I wasn't sure we had lost
that guy.

"I can't make it."

"Yeah, you can. Come on."

Steve just shook his head. I told him what
would happen to him if he got caught. I made it
sound worse than falling off the roof. Anyway, it
was only two floors up. I'd dropped off a two-story

roof before and only broke my ankle. I did it on a dare.

"Come on," I said. "I'll catch ya."

Steve looked back at the door, then down at the alley, backed up a few feet and jumped. He didn't know how to do it right at all. But for some reason he made it, landing across his belly on the ledge. He was so surprised he made it that he forgot to hang on and just slipped down. He would have gone all the way down if I hadn't caught his wrist. He hung there hollering his head off, till I said, "If you don't shut up I'll drop you."

I wasn't threatening him; I was just telling the truth. I kept trying to haul him up, but it wasn't easy. I was hurting pretty bad, too.

"And don't look at me like a rabbit, neither," I panted.

He was trying to get a toehold on the wall. He worked so hard to change the expression on his face so he wouldn't look like a rabbit that it almost made me laugh and drop him. Finally, he climbed and clawed his way on up. We just sat there trying to breathe again. I kept listening for that guy who was chasing us. Finally I figured we'd lost him.

"I guess we didn't need to do that," I said. "He ain't comin' up here."

I didn't notice till then that Steve was shaking pretty bad.

"We didn't need to do that, huh?" he said, and really swore at me. I just sat there and tried not to laugh.

"You shouldn'ta throwed them hubcaps away," I said. "I coulda got twenty bucks for 'em."

"You were stealing them." He said it like he was really telling me something new.

"So what. They stole 'em from somebody else."

"That isn't any reason."

I started to answer him, then thought, Why bother? We'd had this argument before.

"You all right?" he asked. I said no, and passed out cold. What with all that running and jumping around and bleeding and not eating anything that day, I was in pretty bad shape.

I wasn't out too long, just long enough to scare Steve into looking for some help, so when I came to I was laying there on the roof by myself. I fixed that as soon as possible, almost running to the roof door. I bumped into Steve and some old lady he'd talked into coming to help. I don't know what the hell he thought she should do. I said, "Let's go," and got out of there. That lady was real unhappy about being dragged up there.

I was so mad at Steve for going off and leaving

me that it took me about three blocks of fast walking to see that he was crying. That scared the hell out of me. I'd never seen anybody but girls cry, and I couldn't ever remember doing it myself.

"What's with you?" I asked him.

"Just shut up," he said. "Just shut the hell up."

Now that wasn't like him at all. I decided he must still be worrying about his mother. I couldn't remember mine, so I didn't know how he felt.

5

Steve went home, and I went home, because I didn't want to keel over in the streets and because I figured the Motorcycle Boy might be there. It was still a little early for the old man.

I ran into Cassandra on the way up the stairs. I mean, really ran into her. Cassandra thought she was the Motorcycle Boy's girl friend. She was a weirdo, if you ask me. I couldn't stand her. See, she'd been a student teacher at the high school the year before, and the Motorcycle Boy was in one of her classes. She flipped out over him. Girls were chasing him all the time anyway. It wasn't just because he was good-looking. He was different-looking. Anyway, he could have any chick he wanted, and what he saw in Cassandra I don't know. He must have been sorry for her.

There she was, college-educated and from a good family and from a nice home on the other side of town, and she moves here into an old apartment and follows the Motorcycle Boy around. She wasn't even pretty. I didn't think so, anyway. Steve said she was, but I didn't think so. She'd walk around barefoot like a hick and didn't wear any makeup. Almost every time I'd see her she'd be carrying a cat. I don't like cats. I didn't go as far as Biff Wilcox did, use them for target practice with a twenty-two pistol, but I didn't like them. And she'd try to talk like the Motorcycle Boy, try to say things that meant something. She didn't fool me.

"Hi," she said to me. I waited for her to move over so I could go on up the stairs, but she didn't. Hell, it was my stairs, for pete's sake. I just looked at her. I never tried to pretend I liked her. "Well, move it," I said finally.

"Charming child," she said.

I said something to her I wouldn't normally say to a chick, but she really got on my nerves. She didn't even flinch.

"He don't like you," I went on. "Any more than he liked any of the rest of them."

"He doesn't like me now, period," she said. She held out her arms. They were covered with tracks. She was shooting up. "See?"

I was surprised for a second, then disgusted. "If he ever caught me doin' dope he'd break my arm."

"He's done almost that much for me," she said. She had always seemed stuck-up, like she thought her and the Motorcycle Boy belonged to some superelite club or something. She wasn't so sassy now.

"I'm not hooked," she said, like I was her best friend. "I just thought it might help. I thought he was gone for good."

One thing the Motorcycle Boy couldn't stand was people who did dope. He didn't even drink, most of the time. There was a rumor around that he'd killed a junkie once. I never cared to ask him about it. One day out of the clear blue sky he said to me, "I ever catch you doin' dope I'll bust your arm." And he'd do it, too. Since that was one of the few times he ever paid any attention to me, I took it serious.

I looked away from Cassandra and spit over the railing. There was something about her that really got on my nerves. She took the hint and went on down the stairs. I found the Motorcycle Boy in the apartment, sitting on the mattress against the wall. I asked him if there was anything to eat in the house, but he didn't hear me. I'd gotten used to that, his hearing had been screwed up for years. He was color-blind, too.

I found some crackers and sardines and milk. I ain't picky. I like about anything. I also found a bottle of sneaky pete and finished it off. The old man never kept count.

I took off my shirt and washed out my knife cut again. It hurt real steady, not bad, but steady, like a toothache. I'd really be glad when it quit hurting.

"Hey," I said to the Motorcycle Boy, "don't go anywhere till the old man gets home, okay?"

He dragged his eyes off the wall, looked at me slowly without changing his expression, and I could tell he was laughing.

"Poor kid," he says to me, "looks like you're messed up all the time, one way or another."

"I'm okay," I said. I was a little surprised he'd worry about me. See, I always thought he was the coolest guy in the world, and he was, but he never paid much attention to me. But that didn't mean anything. As far as I could tell, he never paid any attention to anything except to laugh at it.

My father came in after a while.

"Both of you are home?" he asked. He wasn't as drunk as usual.

"Hey, I need some money," I told him.

"I haven't seen you for quite some time," the old man said to the Motorcycle Boy.

"I was home last night."

"Indeed. I didn't notice." My father talked funny. He'd been to college. Law school. I never told anybody that because nobody'd believe it. It was hard for me to believe it myself. I didn't think people who went to law school turned into drunks on welfare. But I guess some of them did.

"I need some money," I repeated.

He looked at me thoughtfully. Me and the Motorcycle Boy didn't look anything like him. He was a middle-sized, middle-aged guy, kind of blond and balding on top, light-blue eyes. He was the kind of person nobody ever noticed. He had a lot of friends, though, mostly bartenders.

"Russel-James," he said suddenly. "Are you ill?"

"Got cut up in a knife fight," I told him.

"Really?" He came over to take a look. "What strange lives you two lead."

"I ain't so strange," I said.

He gave me a ten-dollar bill.

"And how about you?" he asked the Motorcycle Boy. "Did you have a nice trip?"

"Yeah. Went to California."

"How was California?"

"It was one laugh after another. Even better than here, as amusing as this place is." The Motorcycle Boy looked straight through the old man, seeing something I couldn't see.

I was hoping they wouldn't get started in on one of their long talks. Sometimes they'd go for days like they didn't even see each other, and sometimes they'd get started on something and talk all night. That wasn't much fun for me, since I couldn't understand half of what they said.

It was hard for me to decide exactly how I felt about my father. I mean, we got along okay, never had any kind of arguments, except when he thought I'd been swiping his wine. Even then he didn't mind much. We didn't talk any, either. Sometimes he'd ask me a question or something, but I could tell he was just trying to be polite. I'd tell him about a river bottom party or a fight or a dance, and he would just look at me like he didn't understand English. It was hard for me to respect him, since he didn't do anything. He drank all day out in bars, and came home and read and drank at night. That's not doing anything. But we got along okay, so I couldn't hate him or anything. I didn't hate him. I just wished I could like him better.

I think, though, he liked me better than he did the Motorcycle Boy. He reminded the old man of our mother. She left a long time ago, so I didn't remember her. Sometimes he'd just stop and stare at the Motorcycle Boy like he was seeing a ghost.

"You are exactly like your mother," he'd tell him. And the Motorcycle Boy would just look at him with that blank, expressionless animal face.

The old man never said that to me. I must look like her, too, though.

"Russel-James," my father said, settling down with a book and a bottle. "Please be more careful in the future."

The Motorcycle Boy was quiet for so long I finally thought he was upset about Cassandra.

"She said she wasn't hooked," I told him. Even though I didn't like her, I thought maybe this would cheer him up.

"Who?" he asked me, surprised.

"Cassandra."

"Oh, yeah. Well, I believe her."

"You do?"

"Sure. You know what happened to people who didn't believe Cassandra."

I didn't. My father said, "The Greeks got 'em."

Now see what I mean? What the hell did Greeks have to do with anything?

"You don't like her anymore, though, huh?" I asked him.

He didn't answer me. He just got up and left. I went to sleep right away. Smokey came by around midnight with his cousin who had a car, so I went to the lake and drank beer with them. There were some girls there and we built a fire and went swimming. When I got home it was early in the morning. The old man woke up and said, "Russel-James, I heard a rumor going around that a policeman was determined to get one of you. Is it you or your brother?"

"Both of us, but mostly him."

I knew who he meant. The cop was a local who had hated us for years. I wasn't worried about that. I was a little worried that I might have got my side infected from swimming in the lake, but it looked all right.

I was tired again, so I cut school and slept till noon.

6

That afternoon turned out to be more interesting than I'd bargained for. I got expelled, and Patty broke up with me.

I went to school about one o'clock. I had to check in at the office and let them know I was there. I told them I had been sick that morning but was okay now. They didn't believe me, but I wasn't going to say I'd been to a beer blast till five in the morning.

I had done the same thing lots of times before, so I was surprised when, instead of giving me a pass back to class, I was sent in to see Mr. Harrigan, the guidance counselor.

"Rusty," he said, shuffling through some papers

on his desk to let me know I was taking up his valuable time. "You have been to see me before."

"Yeah," I said. I can't stand for people to call me just "Rusty." It makes me feel like I'm not wearing my pants or something.

"Too many times," he said.

I was wondering what was coming. I mean, I didn't go in there and waste his time on purpose. All they had to do was quit sending me there.

"We have decided that we can no longer tolerate your kind of behavior." He went on to list all the things I'd been sent to the office for that year: fighting, swearing, smoking, sassing the teacher, cutting classes ...

It was quite a list, but I already knew about it. He acted like he was telling me something I didn't know about. My mind went kind of blank. There was something about Mr. Harrigan that made my mind go kind of blank, even when he was swatting me with a board, like he had two or three times before.

All of a sudden I realized he was kicking me out of school.

"We have arranged for you to be transferred to Cleveland," he was telling me. Cleveland High was the school where they sent everybody they didn't like. That didn't bother me. But Biff Wilcox and his gang ran Cleveland. Since our fight, Biff and me had left each other alone. He stayed in his neighborhood, I stayed in mine. But if I just walked into his home territory, I was a dead man. It'd be me against half the school. Biff had had his chance to fight me fair. He wasn't going to try that again. Sure, I'd go to Cleveland. All I needed was a submachine gun and eyes in the back of my head.

"I don't want to go," I said. "Look, I done lots of things worse than cutting school for half a day. Why now?"

"Rusty," he said, "they are equipped to handle your kind in Cleveland."

"Yeah? They got bars on the windows and bullet-proof vests?"

He just looked at me. "Don't you think it's time you gave some serious thought to your life?"

Well, I had to worry about money, and whether or not the old man would drink up his check before I got part of it, and whether or not the Motorcycle Boy would pick up and leave for good, and I had a cop itching to blow my brains out. Now I was getting sent to Biff Wilcox's turf. So I didn't have much time for serious thinking about my life.

I gave some serious thought about punching

Mr. Harrigan. I mean, they were kicking me out anyway. But I was still a little hung-over, so I decided not to waste the energy.

"You start at Cleveland next Monday, Rusty," Mr. Harrigan said. "You are suspended until then."

"I won't go," I said.

"The alternative is the Youth Detention Center." He rattled his papers again, to show that my time was up.

The Youth Detention Center. Big deal. Those guys had a lot of paperwork to get straightened out before they came after me. I had weeks to think of something to do, before they showed up.

I left his office with the intention of heading straight for his car and slashing his tires. But I ran into Coach Ryan in the hall.

"Rusty-James, man, I'm sorry," he said. He really did look kind of sorry. "I told them you were a good kid," he said. "I told them you never gave me any trouble."

Which was a lie, since I gave him trouble. He just tried to laugh it off.

"But it didn't do any good. I couldn't talk them out of it."

"Don't worry about it," I told him. He looked at me like I had been sentenced to death. He must have really thought I loved that school. I didn't, but my friends were there, and it was easier to go to than someplace where Biff Wilcox's friends were.

"Kid," he said to me, "don't go getting into trouble, okay?"

I must have looked at him like he was nuts, because he went on: "I mean trouble you can't handle."

"Sure," I said, and added "man."

It made him so happy. I hoped to hell when I was grown I'd have better things to do than hang around some tough punk, hoping his rep would rub off on me.

It really felt weird not being able to stay in school. I had always found something to do in the summer, though, and over Christmas, so I figured I'd get along.

Nobody was in Benny's besides Benny, and even though he was better than nobody, I don't like shooting pool without an audience. I went down the street and over a couple of blocks to Eddie & Joe's Bar. A couple of guys who used to be in the Packers hung out there. But as soon as I went in, Joe (or maybe Eddie) threw me out. Then I tried Weston McCauley's place. He was there, with some other people, but they were all spacey and nervous and dopey, doing horse. Junkies can't stand to be around straight people, so I left, feeling really sad because Weston had been second lieutenant in the Packers. He had been the closest thing to a friend that the Motorcycle Boy had. The Motorcycle Boy didn't have any friends, I realized when I got over being sad about Weston. He had admirers and enemies, but I'd never heard anybody claim to be his friend.

Then it was time for Patty to be getting home from school. She went to an all-girl Catholic school. Her mother didn't want her to be around boys. Patty thought this was really funny. She was the kind of girl who had boy friends when she was nine.

I waited for her at the bus stop, smoking a cigarette and fooling around, smarting off to people passing by. You'd be surprised at how many people are afraid of a fourteen-year-old kid.

Patty hopped off the bus and went swinging on by me like she didn't even see me.

"Hey," I said, dropping my cigarette and running a couple of steps after her, "what's up?"

She stopped sharply, glared at me, and really told me what I could do.

"What's with you?" I asked her. I was getting mad, myself.

"I heard all about your little party," she said. I must have looked as blank as I felt. She went on: "Up at the lake. Marsha Kirk was there. She told me all about it."

"So what? What does that have to do with anything?"

"Do you really think you can treat me like that?" She started off swearing at me again. I wondered where she'd learned to swear so good, then remembered she'd been going with me for five months.

"What does a dumb party have to do with anything?"

"I heard all about you and that girl, that black-haired tramp." She was so mad she couldn't even speak for a second.

"Just get lost," she said finally. Her eyes were shooting sparks. "I don't want to ever see your face again."

"Don't worry, you won't have to," I told her, and added a few comments of my own. I almost slapped her. Then, when she went stalking on down the street, her hair bouncing on her shoulders, her head up, a tough, sweet little chick, I thought how I wouldn't be going over to her house to watch TV anymore. We wouldn't hug close, trying to make out without her little brothers catching us. I wouldn't have her to hold anymore, soft but strong in my arms.

I couldn't see what messing around with a chick at the lake had to do with me and Patty. It didn't have anything to do with me and Patty. Why would she let something stupid like that louse us up?

I felt funny. My throat was tight, and I couldn't breathe real good. I wondered if I was going to cry. I couldn't remember how crying felt, so I couldn't tell. I was all right in a little bit, though.

I just walked around for a while. I couldn't think of anything to do, or anyplace to go. I spotted the Motorcycle Boy in the drugstore reading a magazine, so I went in.

"You got a cigarette?" I asked. He handed me one.

"Let's do somethin' tonight, okay?" I said. "Let's go over to the strip, across the bridge, okay?"

"All right," he said.

"Maybe I can get Steve to go, too." I wanted Steve to go in case the Motorcycle Boy forgot I was with him and took off on a cycle, or went in some bar where I couldn't go.

"All right."

I stood there and looked at the magazines for a little bit.

"Hey," I said, "what you reading?"

"There's a picture of me in this magazine." He showed it to me. It was a picture of him, all right. He was leaning back against a beat-up cycle, kind of propped up on his hands. He was wearing blue jeans and blue jean jacket and no shirt. He and the motorcycle were against a bunch of trees and vines and grass. It made him look like a wild animal out of the woods. It was a good picture. A photograph that looked like a painting. He wasn't smiling, but he looked happy.

"Hey," I said, "what magazine is this?"

I looked at the cover. It was one of those big national magazines, one that went all over the country.

"Is there anything about you in here?" I looked through the magazine again.

"No. The photograph is one of a collection by a famous photographer. She took my picture out in California. I'd forgotten it. Actually, it was one hell of a shock to open a magazine and find my picture in it."

I looked at the other photographs. They were

mostly of people. They all looked like paintings. The magazine said that the person who took them was famous for her photos looking like paintings.

"Wow," I said. "Wait till I tell everybody."

"Don't, Rusty-James. I'd rather you didn't tell anybody. God knows it's gonna get around soon enough."

He had been acting a little weird ever since he got back. He had a funny look on his face now, so I said, "Sure."

"It's a bit of a burden to be Robin Hood, Jesse James and the Pied Piper. I'd just as soon stay a neighborhood novelty, if it's all the same to you. It's not that I couldn't handle a larger scale, I just plain don't want to."

"All right," I said. I knew what he meant about being Jesse James to some people. The Motorcycle Boy was very famous around our part of the city. Even the people who hated him would admit that.

"Hey, I get it," I said. "The Pied Piper. Man, those guys would have followed you anywhere. Hell, most of them still would."

"It would be great," he said, "if I could think of somewhere to go."

As we were leaving the drugstore, I saw the cop, Patterson, across the street, watching us. I stared back at him. The Motorcycle Boy, as usual, didn't even see him.

"That is really a good picture of you," I said.

"Yes, it is." He was smiling, but not happy. He never smiled much. It scared me when he did.

7

We went downtown that night, across the bridge, to where the lights were. It wasn't as hard to talk Steve into going along as I'd thought it'd be. Usually I had to hound him and stop just short of threatening him to get him to do anything his parents wouldn't like. This time, though, he just said, "Okay, I'll tell my father I'm going to the movies." Which was the easiest time I ever had talking him into something. Steve had been acting peculiar lately. Ever since his mother went into the hospital he'd had a funny kind of empty recklessness to him. He looked like a sincere rabbit about to take on a pack of wolves.

He met us at our place. I never went to his

house. His parents didn't even know he knew me. I poured half a bottle of cherry vodka into a bottle of sneaky pete to take with us.

"Here, take a swig of this," I said to Steve as we went across the bridge. There wasn't much space for walking. You were supposed to drive across. We stopped in the middle so the Motorcycle Boy could look at the river awhile. He'd been doing that ever since I could remember. He really liked that old river.

I handed Steve the bottle, and to my surprise he took a drink. He never drank. I'd been trying to get him to for years, and had just about given up on it. He gagged, looked at me for a second, then swallowed it. He wiped his eyes.

"That stuff tastes awful," he told me.

"Don't worry about the taste," I said. "It'll get you there."

"Remind me to chew gum before I go home, okay?"

"Sure," I said. The Motorcycle Boy was ready to move on again and we trotted along behind him. He covered a lot of ground with one stride.

It was going to be a good night. I could tell. The Motorcycle Boy was basically a night person. He'd come home in the morning and sleep past one or two, and really just be getting awake good around four. He was hearing pretty good, too, and didn't seem to mind us going with him. He didn't use to like me following him around. Now it seemed like he barely noticed we were there.

"Why do you drink so much?" Steve asked me. Something was bugging him. He always was kind of nervous and bothered, but I couldn't believe he'd ever try to pick a fight with me.

"You can't stand your father drinking all the time," he went on doggedly. "So why do you? Do you want to end up like that?"

"Aw, I don't drink that much," I said. I was over into the city, on the strip, where there were lots of people and noise and lights and you could feel energy coming off things, even buildings. I was damned if Steve was going to mess it up for me.

"Man, this is gonna be a good night," I said, to change the subject. "I love it over here. I wish we lived over here."

I swung myself around a light pole and almost knocked Steve into the street.

"Calm down," he muttered. He took another swallow from the bottle. I figured that would cheer him up some.

"Hey," he said to the Motorcycle Boy, "you want a drink?"

"You know he don't drink," I said. "Just some-times."

"That makes a hell of a lot of sense. Why don't you?" Steve asked.

The Motorcycle Boy said, "I like control."

Steve never talked to the Motorcycle Boy. That wine had really made him brave.

"Everything over here is so cool," I went on. "The lights, I mean. I hate it on our block. There ain't any colors. Hey," I said to the Motorcycle Boy, "you can't see the colors, can ya? What's it look like to you?"

He looked at me with an effort, like he was try-ing to remember who I was. "Black-and-white TV, I guess," he said finally. "That's it."

I remembered the glare the TV gave off, at Pat-ty's house. Then I tried to get rid of the thought of Patty.

"That's too bad."

"I thought color-blind people just couldn't see red or green. I read somewhere where they couldn't see red or green or brown or something," Steve said. "I read that."

"So did I," the Motorcycle Boy answered. "But we can't be everything we read."

"It don't bother him none," I told Steve.

" 'Cept when he's cycle-ridin' he tends to go through red lights."

"Sometimes," said the Motorcycle Boy, surprising me since he didn't usually start conversations, "it seems to me like I can remember colors, 'way back when I was a little kid. That was a long time ago. I stopped bein' a little kid when I was five."

"Yeah?" I thought this was interesting. "I wonder when I'm gonna stop being a little kid."

He looked at me with that look he gave to almost everybody else. "Not ever."

I really thought that was funny, and I laughed, but Steve glared at him—a rabbit scowling at a panther. "What's that supposed to be, a prophecy or a curse?"

The Motorcycle Boy didn't hear him, and I was glad. I didn't want Steve to get his teeth knocked out.

"Hey," I said. "Let's go to a movie."

There were some good ones right there on the strip. We were passing the advertising posters.

"That sounds like a great idea," Steve said. "Let me have the bottle."

I handed it to him. He was getting happier every time he took a drink.

"Too bad," he said. "You have to be eighteen

to get into this movie. That is too bad, since it really looks interesting." He was studying some of the scenes they had on the advertising posters.

The Motorcycle Boy went to the ticket seller and bought three tickets, came back and handed us each one. Steve stared at him, openmouthed.

"Well," said the Motorcycle Boy. "Let's go."

We walked right in.

"Was that guy blind or something?" Steve said loudly. In the movie-house dark I could hear people turn around to look at us.

"Shut up," I told him. I had to wait so my eyes could get used to the dark. It didn't take long. The Motorcycle Boy had already found us seats right in the middle.

"I got in here before," I told Steve, "and the place was raided. That was a blast. You shoulda seen the movie they were playing that night. It was somethin' else."

I was going on to tell him about the movie, but he interrupted me with "Raided? Police raid?" He was quiet for a little while, then said, "Rusty-James, if you're arrested or something, can you refuse bail? I mean, can't you stay in jail if you'd rather do that than go home?"

"What are you talkin' about?"

"If my father had to come to the jailhouse and

71

get me, I'd rather stay there. I mean it. I'd rather stay in jail."

"Aw, relax," I said. "Nothin' is gonna happen." I lit up a cigarette and put my feet up on the back of the chair in front of me. Could I help it if somebody was sitting there? The person in the seat turned around and gave me a dirty look. I looked back at him like there was nothing I'd rather do than bash his face in. He moved over two seats.

"That was pretty good," said the Motorcycle Boy. "Did you ever think of trying out for a chameleon?"

"I don't know them," I said, kind of proud of myself. "Where's their turf?"

For a minute I heard Steve trying to smother his laughter. Hell, I could hear both of them laughing, but the movie got started, so I didn't pay any attention.

The very beginning of the movie was just some people talking. I figured it wouldn't be too long before we got to the good stuff, and it wasn't, but by that time Steve wasn't looking at the screen anymore. See, the Motorcycle Boy never watched movies. He watched the people in the audience. I'd been to movies before with him, so it didn't bother me, but now Steve was looking at the people, too, to see what was so interesting. There wasn't anything interesting, just some old men, some college kids, some people who had drifted in off the streets, and what looked like some rich kids from the suburbs, slumming. It was the usual people. I knew that was one of the Motorcycle Boy's weird habits, but I hated for Steve to miss parts of the movie, especially since I was sure he hadn't been to a skin flick before. So I poked him in the ribs and said, "You're missin' out on somethin', kid."

When he looked at the screen he froze. It was my turn to laugh.

"Are they faking that?" he asked in a strangled voice.

"I doubt it," I said. "Would you?"

"You mean," his voice rose slightly, "that people *film* that?"

"Naw, this is live from Madison Square Garden. Sure, they film it."

He sat there for a few minutes more, then jumped up hurriedly.

"I gotta go to the john," he said. "I'll be right back."

"Steve!" I hollered at him, but he was gone. After about ten minutes I knew he wasn't coming back.

"Come on," I said to the Motorcycle Boy. Outside it was almost as dark as in the movie house, until you got used to the colored lights. I found Steve plastered up against a wall, a sick look on his face.

"Well," I said. "What happened?"

"Nothing. I don't know. A guy just asked me if I liked the movie. What's scary about that?"

It was like he was talking to himself.

"I was gonna tell you." I took the wine bottle out of my black leather jacket. "You never go to the john in those places. I mean, never."

Steve gave me a startled look. "So it *was* scary? I didn't just make it up—I mean, is there really something to be scared of?"

"Yep," I said. Steve looked like he was going to throw up. I thought another drink might help him. It did seem to perk him up some.

"I didn't mean to make you guys miss the movie," he said.

"We ain't missin' nothin'. I seen better."

We went down the block. The Motorcycle Boy turned to walk backwards a few steps.

"Sin City," he read the theater marquee cheerfully. "Adults Only."

We went bopping on down the street. The street was jammed with cruising cars. You could hear music blasting out of almost every bar. There were lots of people.

"Everything is so cool . . ." I waved my cigarette at the noise. I couldn't explain how I felt. Jivey, juiced up, just alive. "The lights, I mean, and all the people."

I tried to remember why I liked lots of people. "I wonder—how come? Maybe because I don't like bein' by myself. I mean, man, I can't stand it. Makes me feel tight, like I'm bein' choked all over."

Neither one of them said anything. I thought maybe they hadn't even heard me, but all of a sudden the Motorcycle Boy said, "When you were two years old, and I was six, Mother decided to leave. She took me with her. The old man went on a three-day drunk when he found out. He's told me that was the first time he ever got drunk. I imagined he liked it. Anyway, he left you alone in the house for those three days. We didn't live where we do now. It was a very large house. She abandoned me eventually, and they took me back to the old man. He'd sobered up enough to go home. I suppose you developed your fear of being alone then."

What he was saying didn't make any sense to me. Trying to understand it was like trying to see through fog. Sometimes, usually on the streets, he talked normal. Then sometimes he'd go on like he was reading out of a book, using words and sentences nobody ever used when they were just talking.

I took a long swallow of wine. "You . . ." I paused, then started again: "You never told me that."

"I didn't think it would do you any good to find out."

"You told me now." Something nagged at the back of my mind, like a memory.

"So I have." He stopped to admire a cycle parked on the street. He looked it over very carefully. I stood there fidgeting on the sidewalk, zipping the zipper of my jacket up and down. That was a habit I had. I had never been afraid of the Motorcycle Boy. Everybody else was, even people who hated him, even people who said they weren't. But I had never been afraid of him till now. It was an odd feeling, being afraid of him.

"You got anything else to tell me?"

The Motorcycle Boy looked up. "Yeah, I guess I do," he said thoughtfully. "I saw the old lady when I was out in California."

I almost lost my balance and fell off the curb. Steve grabbed hold of my jacket to steady me, or maybe himself. He was swaying a little, too.

"Yeah?" I said. "She's in California? How'd you know that?"

"I saw her on television."

For a second I looked around, trying to make sure everything was real, that I wasn't dreaming or flipped out. I looked at the Motorcycle Boy to make sure he hadn't suddenly gone nuts. Everything was real, I wasn't dreaming, and the Motorcycle Boy was watching me with the laughter shining dark out of his eyes.

"Yeah, I was sitting in a comfortable bar, having a cold beer, minding my own business, watching one of those award shows. When the camera went over the audience, I saw her. I thought I could find her if I went to California, and I did."

It was hard for me to understand what he meant. Our mother—I couldn't remember her. It was like she was dead. I'd always thought of her as being dead. Nobody ever said anything about her. The only thing I knew was the Motorcycle Boy— my father telling the Motorcycle Boy, "You are exactly like your mother." I thought he meant she had wine-colored hair and midnight eyes and maybe she was tall. Now, all of a sudden I thought maybe he didn't mean just *look* like her.

I felt the sweat break out in my armpits and

trickle down my back. "Yeah?" I said. I think, maybe, if the street had caved in under me, or the buildings around us had exploded, I would have stood there sweating and saying, "Yeah?"

"She's living with a movie producer, or was then. She was planning on moving in with an artist who lived in a tree house up in the mountains, so she may be there now."

"She glad to see you?"

"Oh, yeah. It was one of the funniest things she'd ever heard of. I'd forgotten we both had the same sense of humor. She wanted me to stay out there with her. California was very funny. Even better than here."

"California's nice, huh?" I heard myself asking. It didn't seem like me talking.

"California," he said, "is like a beautiful wild kid on heroin, high as a kite and thinking she's on top of the world, not knowing she's dying, not believing it even if you show her the marks."

He smiled again, but when I said, "She say anything about me?" he went deaf again, and didn't hear.

"He never told me about her," I was saying to Steve. The Motorcycle Boy was ahead of us, slipping through the crowd easily, nobody touching him. Steve and me pushed and shoved at people, getting sworn at, occasionally punched. "I never bugged him about it. Hell, how was I to know he could remember anything? Six ain't old enough to remember stuff. I can't remember anything about being six."

An old drunk guy was creeping along in front of us. I couldn't stand for him to be blocking the way like that. It made me mad, and I slammed my fist into his back and shoved him into the wall.

"Hey," Steve said. "Don't do that."

I stared at him, almost blind from being so mad. "Steve," I said with effort, "don't bug me now."

"All right. Just don't go pounding on people."

I was afraid if I hit him or something he'd go home, and I didn't want to be left with the Motorcycle Boy by myself, so I said "Okay." Then, because I couldn't get it out of my mind I went on: "You'd think it'd cross his mind to tell me he saw her when he went to California. I woulda told him, if it was me. That is something he shoulda told me."

The Motorcycle Boy had stopped to talk to somebody. I didn't know who, and I didn't care. "What is the matter with you?" I asked him. I didn't see why he had to go around messing everything up. I felt like the whole world was messed up.

"Nothing," he said, walking on. "Absolutely nothing."

Steve laughed, crazy-like. We stopped to pass the bottle back and forth again. Steve leaned on a glass store window.

"I'm dizzy," he said. "Am I supposed to be dizzy?"

"Yeah," I told him. I was trying to shake off my bad mood. Here I was, having a good time, having a really good time, and I shouldn't let people mess things up for me. So what if the Motorcycle Boy saw our mother? Big deal.

"What the hell." I straightened up. "Come on."

We ran and caught up with the Motorcycle Boy. I started clowning around, trying to pick up girls, trying to start fights, just giving people trouble in general. It was a lot of fun. I might have had a really good time, except for Steve, who was scared, giggling, or throwing up. And except for the way the Motorcycle Boy was watching me, amused but not interested. After an hour Steve sat down in a doorway and bawled about his mother. I felt bad for him and patted him on the head.

We found a party later. Somebody leaned out of a window and yelled, "Come on up, there's a party." There was more booze there, music and girls. I found Steve in a corner making out with a cute little chick about thirteen years old. "Way to go, man," I said.

Steve looked at me dazedly and said, "Is this real? Is this real?" and seemed terrified when he realized he wasn't dreaming.

It did seem like a dream, sort of. Even if we hadn't been drinking so much, I think it would have seemed like a dream.

Later we were back on the streets, and the lights and the noise and the people were more and more and more. Everything was throbbing with noise and music and energy.

"Everything is so bright," I said, looking at the Motorcycle Boy. "It's too bad you can't see what it's like."

8

We were watching the Motorcycle Boy play pool.
I didn't exactly know where we were, or how we
got there, but I knew how long we'd been there—
forever. The place was smoky and dark and full
of black people. This didn't bother me, and it
didn't seem to bother Steve either. Steve and me
were sitting in a booth. The table was scarred and
the plastic covering on the seats was ripped and
leaking cotton junk. Steve was adding to the carv-
ing on the table. He was writing a word I didn't
even know he knew.

"My, my, my," said the guy who was playing
the Motorcycle Boy. "Ain't he fine?"

The Motorcycle Boy was winning. He walked

around the table, measuring his shot. In the dim smoky light he looked like a painting.

"Yeah," I said. "And I'm gonna look just like him."

The black cat paused and looked me over. "No you ain't, baby. That cat is a prince, man. He is royalty in exile. You ain't *never* gonna look like that."

"Whadda you know?" I muttered. I was tired.

"Pass me the wine," Steve said.

"There ain't any more."

"That," he said, "is the most depressing thing I have ever heard."

The Motorcycle Boy won the game and they started in on another.

"Isn't there anything he can't do?" Steve grumbled. He dropped his head on the table and held on to the edges, like he was trying to keep it from spinning around. I leaned my head back and closed my eyes for a second. When I opened them, the Motorcycle Boy was gone. It occurred to me that this wasn't a particularly cool place to be, if he wasn't there.

"Come on," I said, and shook Steve. "Let's go."

He staggered out with me. It was dark. Really dark. There wasn't any lights or people and very little noise. That was kind of spooky, like things whispering around in the dark.

"I'm gonna be sick again," Steve said. He had already puked twice that night.

"Naw you ain't," I said. "You haven't drunk enough."

"Whatever you say."

The night air was sobering him up some. He looked around.

"Where are we? Where's the living legend?"

"He musta took off," I said. It wasn't any more than I expected. He probably forgot we were with him. I could feel the hairs of my neck starting to bristle, like a dog's.

"Hell," I said. "Where'd everybody go?"

We started moving down the street. I wasn't sure about where we were, but it seemed like we ought to be going toward the river. I had a good sense of direction. I was usually right about what direction to go in.

"How come we're walking down the middle of the street?" Steve asked after a few minutes.

"Safer," I said. I guess he thought we should be trotting down the sidewalk, when God knows what was waiting in the doorways. Sometimes Steve was really dumb.

I kept thinking I saw something moving, out of

the corner of my eye, but every time I turned around, it was just a shadow laying black against a doorway or an alley. I started through the alleys, looking for shortcuts.

"I thought we were sticking to the streets," Steve whispered. I didn't know why he was whispering, but it wasn't a bad idea.

"I'm in a hurry."

"Well, if *you're* scared, I guess I should be terrified."

"I ain't scared. Bein' in a hurry don't mean you're scared. I don't like creepy empty places. That ain't bein' scared."

Steve mumbled something that sounded like "Same thing," but I didn't want to stop and argue with him.

"Hey, slow it down, willya?" he called.

I slowed down all right. I stopped. Two live shadows stepped out of the dark ones to block the alley. One was white. One was black. The black had something in his hand that looked like a tire tool. Actually, it was a relief to see them. I was almost glad to see anybody.

Steve said, "Oh, God, we're dead," in a singsong voice. He was absolutely frozen. I wasn't counting on any help from him. I just stood there, gauging the distances, the numbers, the weapons, like the Motorcycle Boy had taught me to, a long time ago, when there were gangs.

"You got any bread?" said the white guy. Like he wasn't going to kill us if we had. I knew if we handed them a million dollars they'd still bash us. Sometimes guys just go out to kill people.

"Progressive country, integrated mugging," Steve muttered. He surprised me by showing he did have some guts, after all. But he still couldn't move.

I thought about a lot of things: Patty—she'd really be sorry now—and Coach Ryan, bragging that he knew me when. I pictured my father at my funeral saying, "What a strange way to die." And my mother, living in a tree house with an artist—she wouldn't even know. I thought about how everybody at Benny's would think it was cool, that I went down fighting just like some of the old gang members had. The last guy who was killed in the gang fights was a Packer. He had been fifteen. Fifteen had seemed really old then. Now it didn't seem too old, since I wasn't going to see fifteen myself.

Since Steve had said something, I had to say something, even though I couldn't think of anything besides "Bug off."

Now here is a funny thing that happened to me—I swear it's the truth. I don't exactly remember what happened next. Steve told me later that I turned around and looked at him for a second, like I was thinking of running. That was when the black guy clipped me across the head. I can't for the life of me think why I was so slow— maybe it was the booze. But the next thing I remember, I was floating around up in the air above the alley, looking down at all three of them. It was a weird feeling, just floating up there, not feeling a thing, like watching a movie. I saw Steve, who just stood there like a steer waiting to be slaughtered, and the white guy who was acting like he was bored out of his mind, and the black guy who casually glanced across to Steve and said, "Killed him. Better get this one, too."

And then I saw my body, laying there on the alley floor. It wasn't a bit like seeing yourself in a mirror. I can't tell you what it was like.

All of a sudden it seemed like I bobbed a little higher, and I knew I had to get back to my body, where I belonged. I wanted back there like I've never wanted anything. And then I was back, because my head was hurting worse than anything had ever hurt me before, and the place smelled like a toilet. I couldn't move, even though I kept thinking I had to get up or they'd kill Steve. But I couldn't even open my eyes.

I was hearing all kinds of noises, swearing and thumps like people were being clubbed to death, and Steve screaming, "They killed him!" Even though I was glad he was still alive, I wished he wouldn't yell. Noises went right through my head like knives.

Somebody pulled me up, and I was half sitting, half leaning against him.

"He ain't dead."

It was the Motorcycle Boy. I would know his voice anywhere. He had a funny voice for somebody as big as he was—kind of toneless, light and cold.

"He ain't dead," he repeated, sounding more surprised that he was glad about it than anything else. Like it had never occurred to him that he loved me.

He had settled back, me against his shoulder, and I heard the sound of a match being struck. He was smoking a cigarette, and I wanted one myself, but I still couldn't move. A harsh, breathing kind of sound kept rasping in my ears, until the Motorcycle Boy said, "Will you stop that crying?" and Steve said, "Will you go to hell?"

Everything was quiet, except for street noises somewhere, the sound of rats scratching around and alley cats fighting a block over.

"What a funny situation," said the Motorcycle Boy after a long silence. "I wonder what I'm doing here, holding my half-dead brother, surrounded by bricks and cement and rats."

Steve didn't say anything, maybe because the Motorcycle Boy wasn't talking to him.

"Although I suppose it's as good a place to be as any. There weren't so many walls in California, but if you're used to walls all that air can give you the creeps."

The Motorcycle Boy kept talking on and on, but I couldn't adjust my mind to what he was saying, couldn't understand it at all. It was like stepping from solid ground onto a roller coaster, and while I was still puzzling over one thing, he had gone on to something else.

"Shut up, willya!" Steve finally cried. He sounded worse scared than when he thought we were going to be killed. "I don't want to hear it."

Maybe Steve had understood the words, I don't know. But I understood something behind the words. For some reason or other the Motorcycle Boy was alone, more alone than I would ever be, than I could even imagine being. He was living in a glass bubble and watching the world from it. It was almost like being alone, hearing him, and I tried to shake off the feeling. I moved my head and the pain knocked me out.

He was still talking when I came to again. Nothing had changed, we were still in the alley, only I could feel morning coming on. I was so cold. I never get cold. I was cold, frozen stiff, unable to move, trying to hear the Motorcycle Boy's empty voice.

He was saying that nothing in his life had surprised him so much as the fact that there were people who rode motorcycles in packs.

I tried to say something, but it came out in a grunt that sounded like a kicked dog.

"Rusty-James," Steve said, "you still alive?"

"Yeah," I said. Oh, man, did I hurt. I'd rather be knifed twenty times than hurt like that. I sat up straight, leaning back against the wall, watching things go in and out of focus.

The Motorcycle Boy sat beside me. We had on almost the same outfit. I always got his clothes when he outgrew them, but they never looked the same on me. We each had on a white T-shirt and black leather jacket and blue jeans. I was wearing tennis shoes, he was wearing boots. Our hair was a color of red that I've never seen on anybody else, and our eyes were alike—the same color, at least.

And people never even took us for brothers.

"What happened to those guys that jumped us?" I asked.

"He clobbered them," Steve said. He didn't sound grateful.

"Bashed one of them really good. The other one took off."

"Way to go, man," I said. My head was hurting me until I couldn't see straight.

"Thank you," the Motorcycle Boy said politely.

"You have to go to the hospital this time," Steve said. "I mean it."

"Shoot," I said. "Back when the rumbles was going on—"

"Will you shut up about that!" Steve screamed at me, not caring if noise almost knocked me out. "The rumbles! The gang! That garbage! It wasn't anything. It wasn't anything like you think it was. It was just a bunch of punks killing each other!"

"You don't know nothin' about it," I whispered. I didn't have the strength to do anything else.

Steve turned to the Motorcycle Boy. "You tell him! Tell him it wasn't anything."

"It wasn't anything," the Motorcycle Boy said.

"See?" Steve said triumphantly. "See?"

"You were president," I said. "You must have thought it was something."

"It was fun, at first. Then it got to be a big bore. I managed to get the credit for ending the rumbles simply because everybody knew I thought they were a big bore. They were going to end, anyway. Too many people doing dope."

"Don't say it was fun," Steve said. "It wasn't fun. You can't say it was fun."

"Oh, I was speaking from personal experience," the Motorcycle Boy said. "I must admit that most of them didn't think it was fun. Most of them were terrified when we had a fight. Blind terror in a fight can easily pass for courage."

"It *was* something," I whispered. I felt so tired and sick and sore that I almost wished I was dead. "There was something about it, I remember."

"A lot of them felt that way apparently."

"Yeah," Steve said to me. "You are just stupid enough to have enjoyed it."

"Well, remember," said the Motorcycle Boy, "loyalty is his only vice."

After about five minutes of silence, the Motorcycle Boy spoke up again. "Apparently it is essential to some people to belong—anywhere."

That was what scared me, what was scaring

Steve, and what would scare anybody who came into direct contact with the Motorcycle Boy. He didn't belong—anywhere—and what was worse, he didn't want to.

"I wonder," Steve said wildly, "why somebody hasn't taken a rifle and blown your head off."

"Even the most primitive societies have an innate respect for the insane," the Motorcycle Boy answered.

"I want to go home," I said dully. The Motorcycle Boy helped me stand up. I swayed back and forth for a second.

"Cheer up, kid," my brother said. "Gangs will come back, once they get the dope off the streets. People will persist in joining things. You'll see the gangs come back. If you live that long."

9

My head hurt so bad the next day, I figured I might as well go to the clinic and see a doctor. The Motorcycle Boy had left right after he dropped me off, and the old man left about noon, so I had to go somewhere.

It was a free clinic—you didn't have to pay anything or even give your right name. It was crowded with old people and lots of whining kids and their mothers. I'd been there before, when the old man had a fit of D.T.'s. He didn't have them often, not as much as you'd think.

I got to see a doctor after an hour or so. He was just a kid. I can't believe he was a real doctor. I thought they had to go to school forever.

"I bumped my head," I told him.

"I guess you did," he said. He washed off the side of my head with this junk that smelled awful and burned like hell. Then he stuck a thermometer in my mouth and listened to my heart awhile. I couldn't see what good that was going to do me, but I just sat there and didn't give him any trouble. The doctors here were really nice. The ones that took care of my father had been really nice. I wished I'd known about this place the time I broke my ankle. I would have gone here instead of the hospital. I hate hospitals. I'd rather be in jail. I didn't have anything against doctors, though. It just seemed like a waste of time to go see them. I thought maybe I could get some pain pills, this time.

"You're running a slight fever," he told me. "I want you to go over to the hospital and get some X rays. You 'bumped your head' pretty hard." He grinned at me like he knew I got it in a fight somewhere, like he had seen so much of the same thing he knew that lecturing me wouldn't do any good.

"Nope," I said.

"Nope what?"

"I ain't goin' to the hospital. Just give me somethin' to make it quit hurtin'."

And just as I said that, everything turned kind of gray and this ringing in my ears got so loud I couldn't hear and I had to grab onto the table to keep from falling off.

The doctor straightened me up and said, serious-like, "You are going to the hospital, kiddo."

He left the room for a minute, to get some papers or something, and I got out of there pretty quick. I wasn't planning on any hospital stay. I'd been there before.

I swiped a bottle of aspirin out of a drugstore on the way home and took about seven of them. I felt a little better after that. I knew where I could get some downers that would fix me up fine, but the Motorcycle Boy classified downers as dope. I could always say I got them legit from a doctor, but I doubt that I could fool him. I didn't want to risk it. After last night I'd believe he could cut my throat without thinking about it.

I went by Steve's house on the way home. I knew where he lived even though I'd never gone there. His father had to be at work, though, and his mother was in the hospital, so I thought I'd be safe enough.

He saw me coming up the sidewalk, because he was holding the screen door open when I got up the steps.

"Good Lord!" I said when I saw him. "What happened to you?"

"I was supposed to be home at ten o'clock last night," he said flatly. "I got in at six this morning."

"Your father did that?" I couldn't believe it. I've come out of gang fights looking better than he did.

"Come on in," he said.

I'd never been in his house before. It was real nice, with furniture and carpets and stuff sitting on shelves. It was nicer than Patty's house, but then, she had those little kids tearing up everything. I sat down on a sofa, hoping I wasn't messing anything up. You'd think it would have gotten sloppy, with his mother in the hospital for so long.

"Your father did that to you?" I asked again. I thought maybe I had missed something last night, that those two punks had worked him over. I didn't remember much about the morning, or going home. I think it might have been then that my memory went goofy on me.

"Don't tell anybody, huh?" he said. "I'm gonna say I got it last night, across the river."

"Okay," I said. It was hard for me to imagine anybody hitting Steve, anybody besides me, I mean. I had gone to a lot of trouble making sure nobody hit him. It made me mad. He was my friend. Nobody had any right beating him up like that. What difference did it make if he came home at ten or at six? He got home, didn't he? Why did people get upset about stupid stuff like that? I tried picturing my father beating me up, and couldn't do it. I couldn't even imagine him telling me when to be home.

"He didn't mean to hit me so much," Steve said. But he was just repeating something he'd been told. "He's been worried about Mom. I didn't need to worry him, too. I just didn't think about that."

It was like he had been brainwashed, repeating that stuff. I tried to figure out why Steve wasn't mad about getting knocked around like that. If somebody had done that to me—

"What really set him off," Steve was saying, "was that orange junk all over my shirt. I guess that girl, that girl was wearing a lot of makeup, I guess. I don't remember her being orange."

We sat there without saying anything for a long time. Finally Steve said, "What'd you come over for, Rusty-James?"

I opened my mouth, and closed it, trying to think of the best way to tell him.

"Steve, I think we'd better follow the Motorcycle Boy around for a while."

He said, "Why?" I wasn't ready for that. I was ready to talk him into it.

"Well," I said, "I just think we ought to." I hadn't really thought of why myself. It just seemed like something that needed doing. "I think maybe we ought to watch him for a while, that's all."

"Count me out," Steve said.

"You gotta help me," I said. I had been feeling funny all day. It had started the night before, when the Motorcycle Boy told me why I was scared to be by myself. It sort of felt like nothing was solid, like the street would tilt all of a sudden and throw me off. I knew that wasn't going to happen, but that's what it felt like. And since getting clobbered, everything even *looked* funny, like I was seeing things through distorted glass. I didn't like it. I didn't like it one bit. All my life, all I had to worry about was real things, things you could touch, or punch, or run away from. I had been scared before, but it was always something real to be scared of—not having any money, or some big kid looking to beat you up, or wondering if the Motorcycle Boy was gone for good. I didn't like this being scared of something and not knowing exactly what it was. I couldn't fight it if I didn't know what it was.

"I won't help you," Steve said again.

"Just follow him around for a little bit," I said. He won't go across the river again. He just went last night because I asked him to. He'll stick around here. We won't get into any trouble again."

"I have to go to school," Steve said.

"So meet me after school."

"You don't need me there."

"Yeah, I do."

"Ask B.J. or Smokey."

I started to say, "They'd laugh at me," but changed it to: "Oh, they don't know anything. I mean, they think the Motorcycle Boy's cool and everything, but they don't know him like me and you do."

"You mean they don't know he's nuts."

I jumped up, grabbed him by his shirt front and slammed him back against the wall.

"You don't ever say that!" I shouted at him. I knocked him back against the wall so he'd remember. "You hear me?"

"Yes," he said. I let him go. Then all of a sudden I couldn't see, and the pain was like an awful

noise in my head. I sort of fell against the wall,
trying to get my breath and my vision.

When my eyes cleared up I saw Steve standing
there, worried-looking. His lips were moving, but
I couldn't hear anything. Then my hearing came
back.

"... all right?" he asked.

If it had been anybody else I would have
laughed, shrugged it off and left. But it was only
Steve, and I had known him all my life and I was
just too plain tired to put up a front. Maybe that
was why Steve was my best friend instead of B.J. I
didn't have to keep on being the toughest cat in
the neighborhood for Steve.

I sat down and dropped my head onto my
hands. For a second my throat swelled up on the
inside and I had a sudden picture of Patty bouncing on down the street. That was what I felt like.
Close to crying.

"Steve," I said. "I never asked you for nothing.
I never let anybody punch you around, and I
never bummed money off you. I'm asking you
now."

"Don't," he said. "'Cause I won't do it."

I couldn't talk. If I tried to talk I'd be crying. I
couldn't remember crying. You didn't cry if you
were tough.

"Rusty-James," Steve said. I didn't look up. He sounded like he felt sorry for me and I didn't want to see him feeling sorry for me, because if I did I would hit him, no matter what.

"I've tried to help you," he said. "But I've got to think about myself some."

I wondered what he was talking about.

"You're just like a ball in a pinball machine. Getting slammed back and forth; and you never think about anything, about where you're going or how you're going to get there. I got to think for myself, I can't keep on thinking for you, too."

I didn't understand what he was talking about. Why did all the people I liked talk about such weird things? I did think about where I was going. I wanted to be like the Motorcycle Boy. I wanted to be tough like him, and stay calm and laughing when things got dangerous. I wanted to be the toughest street-fighter and the most respected hood on our side of the river. I had tried everything, even tried to learn to read good to be like him. Even though nothing had worked so far, that didn't mean nothing ever would. There wasn't anything wrong with wanting to be like the Motorcycle Boy. Even Steve admired him—

"You don't like the Motorcycle Boy, do you, Steve? Then why do you think he's cool?"

Steve looked surprised. "Well," he said slowly, "he is the only person I have ever met who is like somebody out of a book. To look like that, and be good at everything, and all that."

That struck me as funny. I laughed and got up to leave. I wasn't going to pester him anymore. Steve walked with me to the door.

"You better go to a doctor," he said.

"I been."

"You better let go of the Motorcycle Boy," he said. "If you're around him very long you won't believe in anything."

"I been around him all my life," I told him. "And I believe everything."

Steve sort of grinned at me. "You would."

" 'Bye," I said.

"Rusty-James," he said, really sincere, "I'm sorry."

"Sure," I said. That was the last time I saw ol' Steve.

10

I spent the rest of the day in Benny's. You could see most of the street from the front booth. If the Motorcycle Boy went by, I'd see him.

In the afternoon, after school was out, people came in. I didn't feel like playing pool, but I got a big audience when I started telling everybody about the wild night we had. It made me feel better to tell everything—about the party and movie and bars and pool games and almost-fights and just-missed chicks, and then the mugging and the way the Motorcycle Boy had rescued us. Maybe I told it a little better than it happened—a couple of people gave me looks like they didn't believe *everything.* But there was a lump on the side of my head half the size of a baseball, and when they saw Steve they'd believe it sure enough.

I liked telling things that happened to me. It took the scare out, like it was just an exciting movie I'd seen.

Patty came in. She hardly ever came to Benny's, usually just on her mother's day off. We had never gone there when we were going together because I didn't like other guys looking at her. See, the kind of girls who hung out at Benny's were tough chicks—pretty good girls, you know, but not exactly like I thought of Patty.

"You lookin' for me?" I asked her. It figured she'd want to make up with me. Well, I'd let her sweat it a little bit, like I had been doing.

"Nope," she said coolly. She bought a Coke from Benny and sat down in a booth, looking around like she was looking for somebody. And it wasn't me.

Pretty soon Smokey Bennet came in and slid into the booth next to her. Both of them sat there like I was supposed to pin a medal on them. Everybody got quiet, expecting me to toss Smokey through the front window and slap Patty's teeth out. I admit I thought about it. I thought about quite a few things, watching the crummy pool game. Both guys shooting were so nervous they couldn't play worth anything.

"Smokey," I said finally. "You want to step outside with me?"

"I ain't gonna fight you, Rusty-James."

"What makes you think I want to fight? Just step outside a minute so we can talk."

"It wouldn't be fair, now," he said. "You ain't in any condition to fight."

"I said I didn't want to fight. Talk—get it? Speak. Communicate."

He looked at Patty, puzzled. But she was looking at me. She still loved me, I could tell. She'd never say so, any more than I'd tell her I still loved her. What a weird thing that was. It was all over, whether we wanted it to be or not.

"All right," Smokey said. He followed me outside, and as the door closed behind us I could hear everybody yapping at once. And a couple of guys were standing on the booth seats, making sure they weren't going to miss anything.

We walked across the street and sat down on a stoop. Smokey lit a cigarette and offered me one. He was still a little tense, like he thought I was going to jump him any second. But he was calm, too, like he thought he could handle it if I did. I wondered why that didn't make me mad.

"Smokey," I said. "Tell me somethin'. The other night, when we went to the lake with your cousin, and those girls were there—did you plan for it to get back to Patty? I mean, did you think this was what was goin' to happen? That Patty would break up with me and you'd move in and maybe take over while I was still done in from that knife fight?"

"Well," he said, slowly, quiet-like, "I guess I did. I kind of thought about it."

"That was real smart," I said. "I wouldn't of been able to think of something like that."

"I know," he admitted. Then he said, "Rusty-James, if there was still gangs around here, I'd be president, not you."

I couldn't believe that. I was the toughest guy in the neighborhood. Everybody knew that.

"You'd be second lieutenant or somethin'. See, you might make it a while on the Motorcycle Boy's rep, but you ain't got his brains. You have to be smart to run things."

I just sighed. I wondered where my temper was. I had a mean temper. I just didn't seem to be able to find it anywhere.

"Nobody'd follow you into a gang fight," he went on. "You'd get people killed. Nobody wants to get killed."

"I guess that's true," I said. Nothing was like I thought it was. I had always thought that one and one made two. If you were the toughest, you were the leader. I didn't understand why things had to get complicated.

"Do you really like Patty?" I asked.

"Yeah," he said. "Even if she wasn't your chick I'd still like her."

"Okay," I said. He went back into Benny's. He was the number one tough cat now. If I wanted to keep my rep I'd have to fight him, whether I was in any shape to or not. He had been counting on that. Everything was changed.

I sat there awhile. B.J. Jackson came by, saw me, and sat down. I was glad to see him. He didn't know everything was changed. I could still talk to him like always. Once he went into Benny's, it would be Smokey he'd listen to. It would be Smokey that everybody would be listening to and watching. It was like this would be the last I could really talk to B.J.

"Guess what," he says. "You know who we had for a substitute teacher today in history? Cassandra, the Motorcycle Boy's chick."

"No kiddin'?" I asked. I guess she had been right, about not being hooked.

"Yeah. Man, we really gave her a hard time,

too. You couldn't pay me a million dollars to be a sub. She was pretty good about it, though. I stayed after class and talked to her some. I says, 'I'm surprised to see you again.' And she says, 'Did you think I'd throw myself off the bridge, or O.D. on a roof or something?' And she told me to tell you something. She said, 'Tell Rusty-James that life does go on, if you'll let it.' Do you know what she meant?"

"Nope," I said. "She was always talkin' crazy. She was a real dingbat."

"I always thought she had a lot of class," B.J. said. He didn't know anything about women.

"You seen the Motorcycle Boy around?" I asked him.

"Yeah, he's in the pet store."

"Pet store? What's he doin' in there?"

B.J. shrugged. "Lookin' at the fish, as far as I could tell. I heard he messed up a couple of guys across the river last night."

"Yeah, he stomped these two creeps that jumped me an' Steve. Almost killed them."

"I heard that. He better be careful, Rusty-James. You know that cop Patterson is just looking for an excuse to get him."

"He's been after the both of us for years."

"You know," B.J. said, "Patterson has the rep

of a good cop. I mean, the Motorcycle Boy is his only bad point. He's never gone out of his way to hassle the rest of us."

"He beat me up once," I said. "And got me thrown into Juvenile Hall for a weekend." I figured Patterson was the only person in the world who thought I looked like the Motorcycle Boy. "Anyway, he's never done so much as say a word to the Motorcycle Boy. He'll never get anything on him."

"Come on," B.J. said. "Let's go get a Coke."

"Naw," I said.

He got up, and started across the street. "Come on, Rusty-James," he said.

I shook my head, and watched him disappear into Benny's. I didn't care if I ever went in there again. And that was a real funny thought, because I never did.

I found the Motorcycle Boy at the pet store, just like B.J. said. He was up at the counter, looking at the fish. They were some new fish, not regular goldfish. I never saw fish like them before. One was purple, one was blue with long red fins and a red tail, one was solid red and one was bright yellow. They all had long fins and tails.

"Hey," I said. "What's up?"

He didn't even look at me. I pretended to be

interested in the fish. I mean, they were pretty and everything, as far as fish go.

"How come they each have a bowl to themselves?" I asked. "I never seen pet fish kept one to a bowl."

"Rumble fish," said the Motorcycle Boy. "They'd kill each other if they could."

I looked at Mr. Dobson behind the counter. He was a nice old guy, a little nuts to keep trying to run the pet store, since all he had were some scroungy puppies and kittens and a parrot that he couldn't sell because we'd taught it all the bad words we knew. That parrot could come up with some interesting sentences. Mr. Dobson looked worried. I wondered how long the Motorcycle Boy had been in there, to scare Mr. Dobson that much.

"That's right, Rusty-James," he told me. "Siamese fighting fish. They try to kill each other. If you leaned a mirror against the bowl they'd kill themselves fighting their own reflection."

"That's really neat," I said, even though I didn't think it was really neat.

"Wonder if they'd act that way in the river," the Motorcycle Boy went on.

"Nice colors," I said, trying to keep up the conversation. I had never seen the Motorcycle

Boy look so hard at anything. I thought Mr. Dobson was going to call the cops if I didn't get him out of there.

"Yeah?" he said. "That makes me kind of sorry I can't see colors."

It was the first time I'd ever heard him say he was sorry about anything.

"Hey," I said. "Let's go boppin' around again tonight. I can get some more wine. We can get some chicks and have a really nice time, huh?"

He went deaf again and didn't hear me. That pet store gave me the creeps, with all those little animals waiting around to belong to somebody. But I stayed there anyway, fooling around until Mr. Dobson said he was closing up. The next day was Saturday, the closest thing to a busy day he ever had, so he closed up and just left the animals there. The Motorcycle Boy stood outside, watching Mr. Dobson close up, until the shades were pulled down over the windows and the door.

And when he finally left the place, I followed him the best I could, even though he didn't even see me anymore. It seemed like the only thing I had left to do.

11

We went home. The Motorcycle Boy sat on the
mattress and read a book. I sat next to him and
smoked one cigarette after another. He sat there
reading and I sat there waiting. I didn't know
what I was waiting for. About three years before,
a doped-up member of the Tiber Street Tigers
had wandered over onto Packer territory and got
beat up and crawled back. I remember waiting
around in a funny state of tenseness, like seeing
lightning and waiting for thunder. That was the
night of the last rumble, when Bill Braden died
from a bashed-in head. I'd been sliced up real bad
by a Tiger with a kitchen knife, and the Motorcycle Boy had sent at least three guys to the hospital, laughing out loud right in the middle of the

whole mess of screaming, swearing, grunting, fighting people.

I'd forgotten about that. Sitting there reminded me. It was much harder to wait than to fight.

"Both home again?" The old man came in the door. He liked to stop in and change his shirt before he went out to the bars for the night. It didn't matter that the one he changed into was usually as dirty as the one he took off. It was just something he liked to do.

"I want to ask you somethin'," I said.

"Yes?"

"Was—is—our mother nuts?"

The old man stopped right where he was and stared at me, amazed. I had never asked him a thing about her.

"No. Whatever gave you that idea?"

"Well, she left, didn't she?"

He smiled slowly. "Our marriage was a classic example of a preacher marrying an atheist, thinking to make a convert, and instead ending up doubting his own faith."

"Don't give me that," I said. "You was never a preacher."

"I was a practitioner of the law."

"Say yes or no, willya?"

"You don't suppose a woman would have to be nuts to leave me, do you?" He just stood there, smiling at me, looking through me like the Motorcycle Boy did. It was the first time I ever saw any resemblance between them. "I married her, thinking to set a precedent. She married me for fun, and when it stopped being fun she left."

And honest to God, that was the first time I came anywhere near to understanding my father. It was the first time I saw him as a person, with a past that didn't have anything to do with me. You never think of parents having any kind of a past before you were there.

"Russel-James," he went on, "every now and then a person comes along who has a different view of the world than does the usual person. Notice I said 'usual,' not 'normal.' That does not make him crazy. An acute perception does not make you crazy. However, sometimes it drives you crazy."

"Talk normal," I begged him. "You know I don't understand that garbage."

"Your mother," he said distinctly, "is not crazy. Neither, contrary to popular belief, is your brother. He is merely miscast in a play. He would have made a perfect knight, in a different century, or a very good pagan prince in a time of heroes. He was born in the wrong era, on the wrong side of the river, with the ability to do anything and finding nothing he wants to do."

I looked at the Motorcycle Boy to see what he thought. He hadn't heard a word of it.

And even though I didn't have much hope that the old man could tell me something in plain English, I had to ask him something else.

"I think that I'm gonna look just like him when I get older. Whadd'ya think?"

My father looked at me for a long moment, longer than he'd ever looked at me. But still, it was like he was seeing somebody else's kid, not seeing anybody that had anything to do with him.

"You better pray to God not." His voice was full of pity. "You poor child," he said. "You poor baby."

The Motorcycle Boy broke into the pet store that night. I was with him. He didn't ask me along. I just went.

"Look, you need some money? I'll get you some money," I said desperately. I knew he didn't need any money. I just couldn't think of any other reason for what he was doing.

"Anyway . . ." I kept on talking, saying anything so I couldn't feel the deadly silence, ". . . if you want money, liquor stores are the best bet."

I stood there, zipping my jacket zipper up and down, wiping the sweat off my hands on my jeans, watching him jimmy the lock of the back door, waiting for something terrible to happen.

"Listen," I said again, "everybody saw you hangin' around here today, like you was casing the place. And a million people musta seen you comin' here. Will you listen to me!" My voice cracked upwards, like it had a year ago when it was changing.

The Motorcycle Boy had the lock on the back door jimmied and he went on in. He turned on the light in the stockroom.

"What are you doin'?" I nearly screamed. "You want the whole neighborhood to know?"

He stood there for a second in the bright glare of the light. He looked calm, his face as still as a statue. He was seeing something I couldn't see. But my father was right, he wasn't crazy.

I watched him let out all the animals. I made one move to stop him but changed my mind, and after that I just leaned against the counter and watched. I had to lean; my knees were shaking so bad I could barely stand up. I was more scared than I had ever been in my life. I was so scared I dropped my head down on the counter and cried for the first time I could remember. Crying hurts like hell.

He let out all the animals and was on his way to the river with the Siamese fighting fish when I heard the siren. I was wiping my eyes and trying to quit shaking. I ran for the door. There seemed to be thousands of red flashing lights in the street. Doors were slamming and people were shouting. I had started for the bridge when I heard the shots.

They tell me there was a warning shot. How did they expect him to hear a warning shot when everybody knew he was deaf half the time? The man who shot him knew it. I was at a dead run at the first shot, and almost to the river by the second. So I was there when they turned him over, and he was smiling, and the little rumble fish were flipping and dying around him, still too far from the river.

I don't remember what happened just after that. The next thing I knew I was thrown up against the police car and frisked. I stared straight ahead at the flashing light. There was something wrong with it. There was something really wrong with it. I was scared to think about what was wrong with it, but I knew, anyway. It was gray. It was supposed to be flashing red and white and it was gray. I looked all around. There wasn't any colors anywhere. Everything was black and white and gray. It was as quiet as a graveyard.

I stared around wildly at the growing crowd, the police cars, wondering why it was all so silent. It didn't look quiet. It looked like TV with the sound off.

"Can you hear me?" I shouted at the policeman next to me. He was busy with his report and didn't even look up. I couldn't hear my own voice. I tried screaming and I still couldn't hear it. I was that alone. I was in a glass bubble and everyone else was outside it and I'd be alone like that for the rest of my life.

Then a pain sliced through my head and the colors were back. The noise was deafening and I was shaking because I was still alone.

"Better get this kid to a hospital," I heard a policeman say. "I think he's in shock or something."

"Shock, hell," somebody replied. I recognized the voice—Patterson. "He's probably on dope or something."

About that time I slammed both fists through the police car window, and slashed my wrists on the glass that was left, so they had to take me to the hospital anyway.

12

"I never went back," Steve was saying. "Did you?"

"No," I said. The sun was shining warm on the sand, and the waves kept coming in, one after another.

"I made up my mind I'd get out of that place and I did," Steve went on. "I learned that. I learned that if you want to get somewhere, you just make up your mind and work like hell till you get there. If you want to go somewhere in life you just have to work till you make it."

"Yeah," I said. "It'll be nice when I can think of someplace to go."

"Come on. Let's go over to the Sugar Shack and I'll buy you a beer."

"I got dried out in the reformatory. Lost my taste for it."

"No kidding? Good for you. I used to worry about that, I remember. I was afraid you'd end up like your father."

"Not me."

"Well, we'll get together for dinner tonight and really go over the good old days. Sometimes I can't believe I've come so far."

I looked out at the ocean. I liked that ocean. You always knew there was going to be another wave. It had always been there, and more than likely it always would. I got to listening to the sound of the waves and didn't hear Steve for a second.

". . . right about that. I never thought you would, but you do. You don't sound like him, though. Your voice is completely different. It's a good thing you never went back. You'd probably give half the people in the neighborhood a heart attack."

I looked at Steve again. It was like seeing the ghost of somebody you knew a long time ago. When he started off across the sand, he turned and waved and shouted, "I still can't believe it! See ya!"

I waved back. I wasn't going to see him. I wasn't going to meet him for dinner, or anything else. I figured if I didn't see him, I'd start forgetting again. But it's been taking me longer than I thought it would.